MRS. MIX UP

CANDACE HARPER

D1478853

MRS. MIX UP

A secret crush. A mix-up in paperwork. And suddenly, a fake marriage that lands two women in one hotel room-- and face to face with their denial.

After six months of simmering attraction, librarians Sofiya Anderson and Molly Andersen are ready to burst. There's a magnetism between them that threatens their commitment to professionalism, and not even a librarian's stern shushing can quiet it down. But they've managed to hold themselves in check...for now.

Until a mistake at a regional conference, a tiny oversight in spelling, makes the coordinators believe they're a married couple.

Two women. One bed. And a Mrs. Mix-Up that doesn't quite go by the books. Can they make it through four days of professional development with both their hearts and their jobs intact?

TRIGGER WARNINGS

I want my books to be a safe haven for everyone who wants them. Therefore, I've included these trigger warnings so that people with phobias, PTSD or general preferences can know exactly what they are getting into.

I have included everything that I could think of to warn for, so please read these and be careful with your mental health, friends.

Sexual: Female masturbation with a sex toy, mention of watching porn, descriptions of cunnilingus and penetration with fingers without condom, and dirty talk.

Non-sexual: Threatened employment, mention of unfriendly divorce of minor character, mentions of aro-antagonist behavior from other queer people, visiting a queer club, coming out as demiromantic, description of a near miss car accident, forced proximity, jealousy, accidental nudity in forced proximity, mentions of queerphobia, mentions of racism, and mentions of sexism.

AUTHOR'S NOTE:

If you are a member of my newsletter or follow me on any social media, you'll know that one of the main characters in this romance novel is on the aromantic spectrum. This is not particularly common in romance novels because a lot of people believe that these things are mutually exclusive. That is very definitely not the case and I think it is something that our beloved genre could do better with when it comes to aromantic and asexual folks like us.

So often, we rely on the typical signals and benchmarks of romantic and sexual attraction to show you exactly how a relationship has progressed towards the "happily ever after" and "happy for now" ending that are vital to the romance genre. Two people meet, they usually experience romantic attraction and a little bit of sexual attraction that they don't act on because it's too early, over time, they fall in love with each other and culminate the relationship with sex, and then they get married. Sound familiar?

However, those signals and benchmarks are often not present or come to pass in a very different order for people on the aromantic and asexual spectrum. Someone on the asexual spectrum may fall in love very quickly but never feel that sexual attraction, or they might only feel it after they've formed an emotional bond or gotten married. Someone on the aromantic spectrum might feel the sexual attraction instantly but never feel anything romantically towards that person, or they might find themselves falling into a queerplatonic relationship that looks like a mix of a romantic and platonic relationship, or they might find themselves falling in love. None of these paths are the same because no two people are the same and no two characters are the same.

As a result, you might find that Molly and Sofiya's relationship hits the "beats" or benchmarks of a relationship a little bit differently than you are used to.

These two women start out hopelessly in lust for each other and the romance comes a little bit later in the story. At the end of this book, there will be a HFN (Happy-For-Now) ending because that is the ending that was right for these two fabulous women.

For all of my aromantic readers, I hope that I have done a good job portraying the aro-spec community. As a fellow a-spec person, I have done my best to make my portrayal as realistic and un-harmful as I can for you to read. Please read the content warnings carefully so you have a heads up about what is coming in this novel.

There will also be an afterword with some recommendations for resources for anyone interested to learn more about aromanticism and books to read by aromantic authors. I hope that you will check them out and take all of this into consideration as you are reading and reviewing Mrs. Mix Up.

DECEMBER 22

SOFIYA

Sofiya felt like she had been filling out paperwork for days, but she'd barely made a dent in the stack in front of her. They shouldn't have taken her that long. She had filled out dozens of these applications in her decade as a reference librarian, and this one was no more complicated than any of the others had been. Yet she kept finding herself distracted by something. Scratch that, not something – someone.

Every few minutes, the new children's librarian would flit into her periphery and then all of Sofiya's focus would disappear into the ether. The impeccably dressed Black woman was reading *Raisin the Littlest Cow*, something that was always a hit with the crowds of children that sat at her feet no matter how many times they'd listened to it.

Even as an adult who had heard the books ad nauseum, Sofiya had to admit that Molly was a captivating reader – and a beautiful one. Not that she would ever admit that last part out loud. It would be entirely unprofessional to say that the tamest of her daydreams were about unfurling the other woman's bun and watching the multi-colored braids cascade down her naked back. As for the rest, well, to say they were not safe for work would have been an understatement.

As if she knew what Sofiya was thinking, Molly glanced towards the circulation desk with the bright smile that would charm even the grouchiest of parents. It made Sofiya melt to her core, thinking of the things she could do to make the woman smile like that. She shook her head, clearing the images from her eyes like a drawing on an etch-a-sketch and trying to hide her blush.

What she found before her was the same stack of papers that would allow Molly and herself to get the funding they needed to attend the regional conference and help them to grow the library's programming even further over the next few years. She needed to get back to work, and so she did. Picking up the next form on the pile, she started to fill it out.

When Molly made an exaggerated movement and laughed along with the story a moment later, the throaty sound sent tingles traveling to Sofiya's most intimate parts. She threw down her pen with a groan. There was no way she was going to get anything done in this room with her body reacting to every sound the other librarian made as if it was straight out of a porno. It all had to get done today so that it was filed before the new year deadline... But where could she go? Libraries were not rife with privacy, especially with how packed it was today.

She racked her brain as she looked around, trying to think of somewhere on the grounds she could go. Not outside, where it had been and would continue raining all week. The library director had been holed up in the office for three days trying to figure out what they needed to ask for during the upcoming budget negotiations, so that was out, too. She refused to sit in the bathroom to do work. That was several steps too far, even for her dramatic self. So, she'd have to look further afield. When her stomach rumbled with what was probably hunger, inspiration struck.

The coffee shop down the street would be the perfect distraction. It would be even more public and she'd have a lot of sounds to lull her into a deeper focus. She could get lunch and talk to Claudia, her friend and barista. They made a killer bahn mi and was a great person. And hey, maybe getting drenched on the walk over would help to figuratively cool her down and get her head back on straight. Well, as straight as a lesbian's head could get.

With resolve, Sofiya gathered up her papers and tucked them into both a weatherproof folder and her briefcase. She stuck her head into the office to tell the director where she was going and headed out into the rain. She could do this. She *would* do this.

MOLLY

"'Your name is Raindrop,' Raisin whispered. 'And tomorrow, I'll help you see over the fence.'" Molly finished. The toddlers at her feet burst into childish applause and she smiled at them. One of the parents had started doing that last week and it had apparently caught on. Not that she minded - it was nice to be appreciated.

Looking around while the parents rounded up their children's things, she noticed that something was different. Isabella had taken over the circulation desk and was waiting patiently. Molly knew she should go and help - it was always a rush when story time let out and the listeners would come and check out their book for the week - but she really didn't want to. She felt like the blood in her veins had been replaced with electricity and it was making her both jumpy and itchy at the same time. It was not a great feeling, but it was one that was increasingly common at this new library.

Not that the library had anything to do with it, really. It only happened on days when she worked with Sofiya, the older white reference librarian. There was something about the lithe woman that drove Molly to horny distraction. Today was the worst day in the six months she'd been working there. The woman's magenta knit sweater hung gracefully over her cleavage in a way that had Molly's heart skipping a beat every time she glanced over. Which was often.

Unfortunately, her usual solution - masturbation - was many hours out of her reach, so she was just going to have to suffer through it. If this kept up, though, she'd have to start packing her vibrator and find somewhere that she'd be able to use it on her lunch break. Her cheeks heated at the thought of the risks that idea entailed, even knowing that it was ridiculous.

As if the universe knew she was thinking naughty

thoughts, a child tugged on the bottom of her wrap dress. Molly plastered a smile on her face and looked down to find one of the smallest boys sucking on three of his fingers with the hand that wasn't wrapped in the dress.

"Hey there, Matt. Whatcha need?"

Instead of answering, he just tugged her dress and started walking towards where his dad stood near the library's double doors. The man stood there watching them with his hands shoved deeply in his pockets. She resisted the urge to groan where the boy could hear it.

"You want me to go talk to your daddy, Matt?" The boy nodded. "Why don't you let me talk to him alone while you go pick out a book to take home? Does that sound good?"

Matt nodded again and scampered off. Andrew Scott was a very attractive, newly single man, which would have been fine and dandy if he had not made it clear to all of the female librarians that he was in the market for a new wife/nanny - and fast. This was going to be awkward at best and his son didn't need to hear her get firm or ugly with him if it became necessary. She *really* hoped it wouldn't.

Let's get this over with, she thought grouchily. Maybe then she could actually do her job.

SOFIYA

It had made sense on the way there, but Sofiya regretted her choice to walk back to the library. The wind and rain left her feeling -and looking- like a rat who had spent way too much time in a frozen lake. The rush of warm air from the library entryway was a welcome change, as was the sight of Molly speaking quietly to one of the parents.

"I'm sorry Andrew, but as my coworkers have told you, we are legally not allowed to date patrons," Molly was saying patiently. Sofiya groaned quietly in sympathy as Molly continued.

She felt bad for the man, because his particularly nasty divorce from the mayor had been fodder for the county papers. However, his flirting technique was terrible, and that was coming from someone who refused to ask her coworker out. It was so obvious from watching them together that he had no idea how to care for his own son.

If he'd had some sense, he'd have waited longer than a week after the ink was dry on the divorce papers and hired an actual nanny to make it less clear that that's what he expected from his partner. One of these days, someone was going to snap on him and embarrass the shit out of him. Sofiya just hoped it would happen in the library so they could all see it. For now, all she could do was rescue poor Molly with a believable, but untrue request.

"Ms. Andersen, I'm so glad I caught you!" Sofiya crowed, throwing her wet coat over one arm. "I need your help filling out some of this grant paperwork so that I can get it turned in before I leave."

She positioned herself right between the white man and her coworker, not obviously enough to be rude but clearly including herself in their conversation. Pure relief washed over Molly's face, but she swiftly hid it behind a sweet smile that revealed none of her true feelings.

"Oh, of course, Ms. Anderson. I can help you with that now. Mr. Scott and I have said everything that needs saying right now. Oh, and I believe Matt's finished choosing his book!"

Sure enough, the boy had a book in one hand and the fingers of his other hand in his mouth while he toddled over. Andrew's face twisted into a grimace, then a smile for his son.

"What did you pick out?" Andrew asked cheerfully. At least he knew better than to make a scene in front of the poor kid. Maybe he was actually a decent person. That would serve him well when he met someone who suited him romantically.

The boy held the book up - one of our many dinosaur books - and Sofiya saw the smile on Molly's face turn from professional into a real one. This one showed a little bit of her slightly gapped front teeth, which didn't seem like a small difference, but it was like the clouds had parted to show off the sun that was her personality. Sofiya was momentarily stunned at how beautiful Molly was, and not for the first time.

Shaking herself out of it and pretending she didn't feel that rush of warmth, she waved to the little boy and tugged her coworker away.

"Are you all right? Do you need a minute to regroup?"

Molly turned her smile to Sofiya and nodded.

"I'm good, thank you. I might go find him a few nanny options, though. This shi—" she cut herself off. "This asking every woman around him to be his girlfriend isn't appropriate."

"No kidding." Sofiya laughed. She was luckily visibly gay enough and old enough that the man hadn't approached her at all, but she'd seen him making his rounds and commiserated with her younger coworkers.

"I'm glad you showed up when you did, otherwise I feel like I'd have had to come out to him to get him to go away and I don't really need that stress in my life."

Sofiya blinked, then raised her eyebrows. That was the first time Molly had said anything about her sexuality in her hearing.

"Is that your way of coming out to me?" Sofiya asked, looking sidelong at the younger woman. Molly's mouth formed an "o" in what she could only guess was surprise. She didn't immediately confirm or deny it. After a moment, Sofiya continued. "You don't have to, if you don't want to. No pressure."

She hadn't meant to make the other woman uncomfortable. She was just curious - a trait that had gotten her in trouble many times before. She'd guessed her coworker was queer, based on her well-honed gaydar and the rainbow-colored braids, but it was always nice to have these things confirmed. *Especially* when that made her wild fantasies a little bit more of a possibility.

"I'll tell you later, okay? I think at least one of us should be helping Isabelle with the crowd." She nodded at the many toddlers crowding around the circulation desk. She was right. A second librarian would be a huge help, Sofiya realized with a grimace.

"Oof, for sure. Want to grab dinner tonight and talk about the conference, too?"

Molly rewarded her with a gap-toothed smile as she turned away. It left Sofiya slightly breathless. God, she hoped she actually was queer - even if it meant she'd have a harder time quashing her inappropriate daydreams. It wasn't like she would act on them unless there was some sign of mutual interest.

Molly took a few steps before she turned back around, a question clear from the wrinkles on her forehead and the frown on her lush lips. "Wait, did you actually need my help with the paperwork?"

Sofiya laughed. "Heavens, no. You're welcome to look over it to make sure I didn't mess anything up, though. You're also welcome to pick the restaurant, if you want?"

"That's all right. I trust you."

The smile came back and Sofiya grinned back while warmth rushed to her cheeks and the tips of her ears. Molly trusted her. That felt good.

MOLLY

By the time the library closed for the night, Molly was dead on her feet. There had been a steady stream of patrons asking for help with various things on top of the kids and teenagers coming in after school to get books before the winter break. It was good to be busy, but man, it was exhausting.

Especially with the realization that she'd sort of accidentally come out to Sofiya earlier in the day. It wasn't that she'd been hiding her queerness, exactly. It was more that her queerness was a little more complicated than most people were willing to deal with, and people's reactions to it were telling. She liked Sofiya and found her incredibly sexy, but she couldn't help worrying about what her reaction would be to finding out that she was a demiromantic lesbian.

For some reason, her being demi was especially a problem with a lot of older lesbians. More than a few had told her she wasn't really queer and thus unwelcome in their spaces. When you added her Blackness to it... well, it got complicated. She guessed that her older coworker was a lesbian, but hopefully Sofiya wouldn't be one of the ones more interested in gatekeeping her than getting to know her. If not, at least she would have plenty of time to lick her wounds between coming out and going back to work. Like most government offices, the library was closed between Christmas Eve and New Year's Day.

A hand closing lightly on her shoulder made her jump, breaking her from her anxious musings. Turning her head, she found herself staring into Sofiya's dancing blue eyes.

"Are you still up for dinner tonight? Today was kind of ridiculously busy."

A smile slid onto Molly's face before she could stop it. She appreciated the out, even though she didn't really need it. Sofiya's thoughtfulness was one of Molly's favorite non-physical things about her, and part of what made her such a great librarian.

"Girl, I am definitely up for dinner. Let me just grab my coat."

Molly could feel Sofiya's eyes on her while she walked back to the main office, so she put a little bit of sway into her gait. If she wasn't looking, it wouldn't matter. But if she was, Molly might as well give her something to look at.

They walked down the street in mostly comfortable silence to the locally owned pizzeria that always gave librarians a discount. They were seated quickly and ordered without looking at the menu - a meat lovers stromboli for Molly and a small supreme pizza with extra mushrooms for Sofiya. By the time the waitress arrived with their water glasses, both women had settled into their booth seats and were chatting about the conference.

"So, have you ever been to a library conference before?" Sofiya drank deeply from her glass and Molly was momentarily distracted by the line of her throat while she swallowed.

"Nope! This will be my first one. I'm pretty excited."

"Ooh, you are in for a treat. Conferences are a lot of fun, but they can get overwhelming quickly if you aren't careful."

"I can believe that just from what I've heard about last year's conference."

Sofiya laughed, a bright sound that reminded Molly of church bells.

"I'm guessing most of those are made up. There is quite a bit of alcohol and some great networking events, but the fun is tempered by panels full of self-important old people and figuring out how to get by without funding for long periods of time. That part is pretty sucky, but it's the reality of library work. On the bright side, since this one is scheduled over the week of Valentine's Day, there are going to be quite a few dating events as well, even for us queers. I guess they don't want all of us to be forever alone like the jokes all claim we are."

Being referred to as a fellow queer made Molly's heart ache in a way it shouldn't have, but the forever alone part... that wasn't something she would have minded. She needed to tell her coworker, so she could at least leave before the food got here if it went poorly. Taking a deep breath, she looked at her coworker, then back down at the bare wood table.

"So, um, about that... you might have guessed that I'm queer, but, um... my identity is a little more complicated than you might expect?" Molly hated that her voice raised an octave and trembled, hated that despite how kind and funny Sofiya was, she couldn't not be nervous saying who she was out loud.

Sofiya smiled softly and twined her fingers together around her water glass, waiting for Molly to continue. She took a drink before she spoke again.

"So, I am a demiromantic lesbian. Do you know what the aromantic spectrum is?" Molly's heart was in her throat and eyes firmly on the table as she waited for the other woman to respond.

"I have heard of it, but I don't know much about what's on it," Sofiya said, her voice soft and slow like molasses "I would love it if you would tell me what that means for you so that I can understand, but you don't have to educate me on everything."

Molly took a deep breath. That was not a bad response. She could do this, just explain a little. She just had to speak as if her heart wasn't about to beat its way out of her chest.

"For me, it means that I don't fall in love with people unless we already have a friendship and make a deep emotional connection. My sexual interest in someone requires very little emotional connection, but I'm only interested in women. And no, that's not the same as being slutty or anything like that. It's just... who I am. "

"Of course," Sofiya agreed. "This is new to me, but I'm glad that you chose to share it with me."

The food arrived shortly thereafter, and they tucked in. Sofiya asked a few questions, but none of them were invasive or gross. Most of them were fairly reasonable. Molly wanted to cry at how well it had gone, but she refused to start crying in the middle of dinner. That was not the adult response to anything.

Just as she finished answering them, a plus sized Latinx person in a black full-length romper swung by the booth with a to-go box. Molly didn't recognize them, but Sofiya clearly did.

"Claudia, long time no see," she laughed. Claudia laughed with her before she explained. "They own and operate The Crescent down the street, which is where I went for lunch today. Claudia, this is my coworker, Molly. She's the new-ish children's librarian."

"Ahh, so this is the Molly you told me about. I see what you meant earlier," they laughed, and a blush spread across Sofiya's round cheeks. Molly wasn't sure what exactly Sofiya had said about her, but the blush said she'd probably like it. Molly wiped the pizza off of her hands, then held one out to the chef.

"It's a pleasure to meet you! I'm sorry I haven't come by your shop yet."

They took her hand in both of their larger ones and grinned.

"You come by anytime, Molly. I'll make sure there's something tasty for you when you do." That last part was said with a wink that she could only interpret as flirtatious. They turned back to Sofiya and spoke again.

"Anyway, there's an after-New Years party at Rosebud's on Tuesday. You should come. Molly, you are welcome if gay bars are your thing. Bring a friend, if you like. We love new faces. I'll see you there, Sof."

Without waiting for an answer or saying goodbye, they sashayed out of the restaurant with a to-go box in hand.

"So, they're quite a character." Molly remarked.

"Oh, you have *no* idea," Sofiya laughed, still blushing slightly. "They've been one of my best friends since I moved here."

"That I can believe. How did you two meet?"

Sofiya laughed again. "That is a story for another day. Now, about the conference..."

SOFIYA

By the time she got home that night, her fingers itched to get onto her laptop. That wasn't unusual. Most days, she watched Netflix while she made herself dinner in her tiny apartment's kitchen or put on one of her favorite porn scenes to relax after a frustrating day, but today was different.

Sofiya wasn't sure what she had expected from the conversation and drinks with Molly, but that had not been it. She had been a member of the queer community for a very long time, but this was the first time she'd been presented with an identity she didn't immediately recognize. It was exciting.

After Molly had come out and explained her identity, they had spent the rest of the evening talking about their coworkers, the programs they had coming up and the plans they had for the future. It had been really nice, even as her brain teemed with questions she knew she should find answers to herself instead of bothering the other woman with them.

So, like any librarian presented with just enough information to get her interested in something she didn't know much about, it was time for her to do some research and make sure she didn't make an ass of herself with the woman who she was beginning to feel things for.

DECEMBER 26

MOLLY

The day after Christmas was a busy one at Molly's house. Her parents had splurged and bought her the couch she'd been lusting after online since she'd moved.

The deep blue velvet tufted sofa was due to arrive any minute, and so was her sister. Her best friend Naomi had driven up the day before to spend the day with her, and she was so excited.

"I can't believe I'm finally gonna have a *couch*," she squealed while looking out her front window. "Can you imagine how much better this place will be with a couch?"

"You mean, with somewhere for someone other than you to sit? No, I can't imagine." Naomi's deep voice was sarcastic with an undercurrent of amusement. Molly wasn't going to react to it. She was more excited than she could remember ever being about a Christmas present, and that was saying something - the Christmas of 2001 when they'd bought her Addy the Black American Girl Doll had reigned supreme in her heart for a very long time.

Plus, it was always great to see her sister. Savannah was a high-level accountant who worked in Raleigh, which meant they got to see each other on a fairly regular basis. Naomi, on the other hand, lived and worked in D.C. They got to see each other a lot less than they did when they'd all lived on the same street in middle school, but that didn't stop any of them from talking to each other daily.

As if she knew she was being thought of, Savannah's Lexus pulled up in front of the house. Molly and Naomi squealed and bolted out the door in unison, racing the still-running car like they were ten years old headed for the ice cream truck.

Savannah, being two years older than the two of them and thus much more mature, completely ignored the women standing outside her car until she had turned the car off and gathered her purse. Then she swung out of the car and swept them both in one motion, wrapping them up in a bear hug with a roaring laugh.

"It's *so* good to see you both. Now get your asses inside before we all freeze to death."

They all laughed and trundled back into the house just in time for the delivery truck to pull up. When two burly white men exited the box truck, Molly pasted on her customer service grin and approached them with excitement.

"Hi, y'all here with a couch for Andersen?"

"We sure are," one man drawled. "Is that you folks?"

"That's me! We've got the space all cleared out for you so you can just set it down in whatever pieces its in and then we'll do the final construction. That way y'all can get on your way."

The men glanced at each other with surprise clear on their faces, as if they hadn't expected her to make this easy for them. She wasn't sure what that was about, but she was ready to make her house feel like a proper home.

"Do you need my signature on anything?"

The man who hadn't spoken glanced at the paperwork and shook his head. "Not until we're done, ma'am. If you'll just show us where you want the couch, we'll get it unloaded for you."

"Well, come on in then!" Molly led them through the door into the almost bare living room. The only furniture in there was a coat rack and a waist-high bookshelf crammed full of her favorites. Everything else was boxes of decorations she hadn't had the energy to unpack

"Where do you want it?"

She pointed to the back wall and both men nodded. They made their way back outside and moments later, Molly heard the telltale clanking and cursing that came with the process of moving heavy objects out of a truck.

Soon, the boxes that held the furniture pieces were where they belonged, Molly had signed the paperwork for the delivery and her house was free of men - as it should be. Now the real fun could begin.

"Okay Google, play my Missy Elliot Spotify playlist on shuffle at volume two."

Get Ur Freak On played first and all three of the Black women started dancing where they stood, just like they had when it first came out in the early oos.

"Let's tackle this couch first, then we finish unpacking the decorations. Sound good?"

The other women danced their way over to where she stood and all three of them got to work.

MOLLY

By the time they had finished with the couch and approximately half of the boxes, they were tired, hungry and sweaty. Luckily, she knew exactly where to take them thanks to Claudia's promise to make sure she was well fed.

The Crescent was bustling when they walked in. Looking around, it was a comfortable sort of space. People were lined up to order and pay, but they were dispatched quickly with a variety of sandwich containers and baked goods that had Molly's mouth watering. In the corner, several teenagers had made themselves at home on the loveseats with their laptops open and were laughing together about something on the screen. It was lovely.

Most of the tables were busy, but Molly spotted a corner table available with just enough space for the three of them, and the benefit of great lighting from two floor-to-ceiling windows. That would be perfect.

"Let me grab a few menus and bring them back to the table. Y'all go sit." She nodded to the corner table and they didn't fight her on it.

"Make sure you get a pastry menu," Savannah told her seriously. "Something in here smells bomb as hell and I'm gonna find out what it is."

Molly laughed. She knew her sister was serious - the Andersen sisters didn't play when it came to pastry. Their chef mother had taught them to love food for what it was, and pastry done well had always been a favorite. Lunch was on her as thanks for all of their help, and she had a feeling she would be spending quite a bit on baked goods for them both to take home. It didn't bother her one bit.

She wove around the people waiting to pay until she reached the counter. The back of Claudia's curvy body was visible through the kitchen window, but they didn't see her, which was fine. She'd rather be friendly to near strangers after she'd had a full meal, which was still a ways away. When she got back to the table, both women were quietly on their phones. Molly could see from the reflections in the glass that Naomi was playing one of those magical merging games and Savannah was scrolling through Instagram. Out of nowhere, she felt a surge of affection for the two women who had always been by her side no matter what.

"I love you guys, you know that?"

Naomi didn't even look up from her phone, just snorted in reply. Savannah looked at her and laughed. "Of course we know that. Now, sit down and share the menus. I'm hungry."

Molly's lips quirked up into a smile as she handed the menus out, pastries first. The table fell back into almost silence as they all read over it. Both the lunch and the pastry menu were full of international foods that were not the customary far in southern Virginia.

"Savannah, did you see-"

"They make alfajores. I need three, ASAP."

The sisters spoke over each other, then laughed together. Naomi rolled her eyes lovingly at them before she spoke.

"You want some real food with that? Or are you just going to eat sugar today?"

"I *guess* that I should," Savannah sighed dramatically. Looking back over the menu, she pointed to one of the lunch entrees. "The caesar salad looks pretty hefty. That'll help balance out the sugar rush, which will hopefully make you mind your own business, *Naomi*.

She stuck her tongue out at the older woman, revealing a small opalescent tongue ring.

"Wait, wait. When did a tongue ring happen?" Savannah squawked. Molly hid a smile behind her menu. She was surprised it had taken her this long to notice the piercing that they had explicitly not told her about. She worked in a position where she had to deal with people at all times and thus had some specific opinions about face piercings.

"For my birthday," she answered nonchalantly. "Now, I can't decide... do I want the banh mi or the bulgogi sandwich?"

"My coworker mentioned the banh mi was really good here," Molly offered while her sister spluttered. "I'm doing the bulgogi, though, so we can split it if you want."

"Sounds like a plan. That makes our order... three alfajores, a caesar salad with the dressing on the side, a banh mi, a bulgogi sandwich and three coffees. Go get them while I explain my piercing to Lady Fancypants here."

Molly did as she was told and a few minutes later, she had a tray full of delicious smelling food and a drink carrier full of coffee and creamer. She was honestly surprised she hadn't seen any of her patrons from the library, but she supposed it was still early yet. They would probably show up when she had a mouth full of food and had to make a fool of herself to say hello. Luckily, the ones who knew her were kids or parents of toddlers, so they didn't care all that much. At least, that's what she kept telling herself.

When she reached the table, the women dug into their food with moans of hunger and delight. It was nearly a solid minute before any of them said anything else.

"So, if she's been hiding a tongue piercing from me, you got anything hidden up those sleeves of yours? A tattoo? A *wife*?"

Molly nearly spit out her food because she laughed too hard.

"No, nothing nearly that exciting. I couldn't even afford a couch. What makes you think I've got the money for a tattoo?"

"I gotta ask," Savannah said airily. "I did notice you didn't say anything about a wife, though. Are you hiding a woman from me?"

That, she had to answer a little more carefully.

"Not... really?"

And with that, she had their full attention.

"What does 'not really' mean?" Naomi asked, apparently not caring that her mouth was full. Her older sister was just staring at her, her dark brown eyes fully focused on Molly.

"I have a crush on one of my coworkers... and I came out to her two days ago? And we're going to a conference together over Valentine's Day?"

"What?" Naomi almost shouted, garnering stares and glares from the people surrounding them.

"Sorry, we're fine! She just got excited." Molly was glad her dark skin barely showed a blush.

"I'm with Naomi. What?" Savannah's face was as loud and pointed as Naomi's voice had been. "Start at the very beginning and tell us *everything*."

Suddenly, Molly felt herself wishing she had just kept her

mouth shut. But, there was very little harm telling them about Sofiya, right? And so she did, not bothering to hide her excitement.

"So, she's a beautiful white woman in her early forties. She's kinda butch but not like super masculine, and her laugh is the most beautiful sound I've ever heard. Wait, I can pull up her headshot from the library website. That'll probably help more than my rambling."

She laughed nervously as she pulled it up. Molly thought it was a beautiful photograph. Her own was not nearly as nice. It showed off the beautiful laugh lines around Sofiya's thin pink lips and her short blonde hair that she was always running her fingers through.

When she was done looking at the picture, Savannah pointed her fork at her younger sister, complete with salad greens and several pieces of cheese. Molly just kept eating her sandwich, waiting for them to ask all the questions she knew was coming.

"What kind of feelings do you have for this girl? Sexual, queerplatonic, or romantic?"

Molly's cheeks were on fire at the question and now she was incredibly thankful no one had come to the table yet.

"Mostly the first one. She's a really nice person, too, so we're kind of becoming friends? I don't know if romantic feelings are gonna happen, but I wouldn't be upset if they did."

"You want to talk about that?" Naomi asked, her voice much quieter than before. They were both watching her seriously now. That was a rare statement from her. She normally found romantic everything to be very overwhelming in a way sexual things never were for her. The alloromantic folks in her life had assured her that usually, things were the other way around.

"No thank you." She wasn't ready for that conversation. She hadn't nearly done enough thinking on what that meant for her. She didn't mind talking about sex in public, but emotions? No, thank you. Luckily, her favorite people knew that. They nodded resolutely and picked up the conversation as if they had never veered into the emotional territory that made her fall into a cold sweat.

"You know, if librarian conferences are anything like accountant conferences, I bet some kinky shit is going on in those hotel rooms," Savannah pointed out. "Maybe you and your new friend can figure out if you're compatible while you're there. After all, what happens at conferences stays at conferences, am I right?"

"I thought the entire point of conferences was to learn things to bring back to your place of work? I don't think figuring out if you're romantically or sexually compatible counts as something to bring back," Naomi said dryly.

Savannah shrugged while she chewed. "It's just as important as learning whatever it is librarians learn at conferences. So what if it's a little more down and dirty than they originally intended? That's what they get for scheduling a conference during the most romantic holiday of the year."

Naomi rolled her eyes and sighed before picking up her sandwich again.

"I'm just saying, the option is there if she wants it. I wouldn't turn down a little hanky panky myself."

"Hanky panky? Savannah, you're a grown woman. You can say the word sex out loud." Molly said with a laugh. "Lords knows we've all heard enough to know you know how to have a good time with it."

Savannah laughed loudly and unashamedly, like she always did when her sexual exploits came up.

"Besides, it's not like she's interested in me. If she was, wouldn't she have said something after I came out?"

"Did she know what being demiromantic was when you came out?" Naomi asked between bites. "I would have done some research before I said anything about being interested. That's exactly what I did when you came out to me, but you know what I mean."

Molly did know. She hadn't known the words she needed back then so she had fumbled through it much more than she had with Sofiya. Afterwards, they had sat together and cried, and then researched more about the aromantic spectrum together. It had been, and still was, one of her most treasured moments in their friendship. It was a pivotal moment and Naomi had made it perfect.

Now that she thought about it, Sofiya's reaction had been pretty much perfect, too. She had said she wanted to do more research, and they hadn't seen each other since that night's dinner...

"Maybe you're right. I mean, we haven't seen each other since dinner that night, so maybe..."

"Did you give her your phone number?" Savannah

nudged her gently under the table. It dawned on Molly that she had not. They worked together five days a week, and she hadn't thought to give the other lesbian her phone number. Her realization was apparently obvious on her face because her companions both began to laugh.

"Lord, child, what are we going to do with you?"

"Love me, I hope?" Molly joked. Savannah and Naomi rolled their eyes in unison.

"Well, that went without saying, you goofball. But you have to give her a chance to say something."

"Give who a chance to say something?" A fourth, accented voice chimed in. All of them whirled around to find Claudia standing beside the table with what looked like samples of every type of pastry in the kitchen. They wore a simple flour-spattered chef's coat over black palazzo pants. The only real adornment was a large enamel pin in the shape of a shield that had they/them carved into it.

"Sorry to interrupt, folks. I'm Claudia, the proprietor and chef here at the Crescent. I knew I hadn't seen any of you in here, though I have met Molly before, and I wanted to greet you properly. Of course, in my world, that means feeding you."

They winked at Molly and grinned at the others.

"How do you know Molly?" Savannah asked, eyes fixed on Claudia's despite the plate of sweets.

"Oh, my friend Sofiya introduced us a few days ago when I interrupted their dinner."

"Oh, their dinner, huh?" Naomi raised an eyebrow at Molly, who flushed. "Molly didn't mention that, but we'll come back to that. We will definitely be taking advantage of that plate, if you don't mind."

Claudia laughed deeply and handed over the plate. Both women pulled pieces off of the plate, then focused back on the chef. Molly didn't know Claudia well enough to say how much they had heard from the table's conversation, but she was suddenly very nervous.

"So you're friends with Sofiya, huh? Molly was just saying she really liked working with her," Savannah said blandly. That's when Molly knew she was in trouble. Her sister was going to draw out every bit of information about the woman she had just told her about. There was no way this wasn't going to go badly.

SOFIYA

Claudia always joked that they didn't give orders outside of the kitchen or the bedroom, and for the last decade of their friendship, that had held true. So, Sofiya knew something was up when she got a text that read simply, "Come to the Crescent ASAP." It had no explanations, no context, nothing.

Normally, she would call them to find out what the hell was going on, but it was the middle of a workday for them. The restaurant business didn't allow any man, woman or enby in charge to take multiple days off, especially during the holidays in a town of 1500. There simply wasn't enough help.

Since she wouldn't be able to reach Claudia even if she called the restaurant, she knew she'd have to go down to the restaurant. And since she didn't know what to expect, she had to change out of the clothes she'd been working around the house in. They were fine for running errands, but if there was any sort of surprise, she wanted to be prepared for it.

Grumbling as she dug through her closet, she pulled out a pair of dark wash relaxed jeans that would easily cover the tops of her favorite boots, a black long-sleeved shirt and a long-sleeved flannel that would keep her warm and as cute as she wanted to be. She dressed up for work or for events that required it, but she preferred a much more relaxed look for her down time.

Pretty much everyone in town had seen her in something similar when she made a grocery store run or went to one of the events downtown. It was unavoidable in a small town, but she realized that Molly was one of the few people she saw regularly who had never seen her at her most comfortable. That led her to wonder what Molly wore on her own days off, and how she was spending the week off. After a moment, she shook her head at herself.

She'd spent the holiday with her brother and his family, which had been wonderful, but she kept finding herself thinking of things that she wanted to tell Molly. They were little things, like her nephews' opinions on the books she'd bought them on Molly's recommendations, but she couldn't because they hadn't exchanged numbers. One would have thought that at the ripe age of 43, she would already know how to get a girl's number when she wanted it.

And yet, there she stood, metaphorically kicking herself for getting stuck in her feelings like a teenager while she got dressed. Maybe it was good that she was getting out of the house. Once again, the walk from her home to the restaurant would do her good and offer her the chance to see everyone's Christmas decorations again before they inevitably started coming down as it got closer to the New Year.

She couldn't help admiring the twinkling lights draped along the roof lines the old Victorian houses and old warehouses that made up downtown Chatham. It made the town seem postcard perfect, but even in that perfection, she could still see the little quirks that made it her favorite place to come home to. The little store that mostly carried local crafts and books with the bright purple tree in the front window, the historic train car that had been turned into a nail salon and painted barn red, and finally, The Crescent.

The corner building had once been a bank and the kitchen was placed in what used to be the vault. The rest of the building was made up almost entirely of glass windows, making it stand out against the worn down red brick that made up every other building in the strip.

One of the windows, she was amused to note, was filled with an eight foot tall croquembouche tower. And there, seated at the corner table with two other Black women, was the back of a woman's head that was very familiar to Sofiya. Multicolored braids swung loose against a soft-looking black hoodie and leggings that she knew would hug Molly's pear-shaped body. At the other end of the table, she spotted Claudia looking in her direction with a huge smile on their face. She was going to kill her best friend.

SOFIYA

Her palms were sweaty and her breathing was coming far too fast for the short walk she had just completed, but she wasn't sure if it was because she was mad at Claudia for pulling a dirty trick on her or because she was nervous about seeing Molly outside of work for the first time or a combination of both. No matter what the reason was, she couldn't just stand out here in the cold forever. She would look like an idiot if Molly turned around, or if one of the other women at the table noticed her and she didn't need any help with that when it came to her crush.

Running her fingers through her hair, she took a deep breath. She was a grown woman. She could manage a chance encounter with her coworker and get a good lunch out of it before she went back into hiding. All she had to do was walk into the cafe and give it the good old college try.

So that is what she did. She walked into the cafe as if she were the most comfortable person in the world, and it didn't take long until she mostly was.

Immediately, she was enveloped in the soft classical music and low buzz of conversation that always filled the room. Despite the floor-to-ceiling glass, she always felt warm and cozy in the room where she had spent many an hour doing paperwork or simply relaxing over a delicious lunch. Suddenly, she didn't feel quite so angry at Claudia as she made her way over to the table.

What harm could come from spending a miniscule amount of time with the woman she was crushing on? Even if she just said hello and wished her a happy holiday, she now knew exactly what Molly wore on her days off. As she stepped closer, she was nearly stunned by just how beautiful the other woman was.

Before she could say anything to the table, Claudia wrapped an arm around her shoulders and beamed.

"Well, look at that! Here's the woman of the hour," Claudia announced, as if they hadn't planned the whole goddamn thing. "Now you can get to know her on your own and I can get myself back to work. We're in for another rush here in about half an hour and I need to be replacing those baked goods."

They winked theatrically and walked away, leaving the table full of shocked faces and half-empty plates. A laugh came bursting up from the depths of Sofiya's belly and out of her mouth before she could stop herself. Before long, everyone else at the table was laughing, too. Other people in the café were staring at them as if they'd lost their minds, but Sofiya didn't care.

"This is what I get for paying attention to cryptic texts. I was just going to grab lunch, but uh, my best friend Claudia is a great chef and drama monarch, apparently. So, uh, hi?"

She could hear herself rambling like a lovestruck teenager

and was absolutely mortified, but what else could she do? Luckily, one of the women sitting at the table saved the day.

"So you're Sofiya, huh?" The slightly older woman at the table looked me up and down, then nodded. "Okay, then. Do you want to join us?"

Before she answered, Sofiya glanced at Molly to make sure it was okay. She was still smiling so deeply she had laugh lines that almost rivalled my own. She gave a small nod without hesitation and Sofiya echoed the motion.

"Sofiya, this is my older sister Savannah and my best friend Naomi. They're both in for the day," Molly introduced her companions.

"It's nice to meet you. We've heard a lot about you."

"Mostly good things," the other woman chimed in. "Are you going to stand there forever or are you going to join us?

Savannah pulled out the chair next to her and Sofiya sat in it carefully. Molly hid her face in her hands while she laughed at the other women's antics. Sofiya had no clue what she had just gotten herself into, but she was certainly into something.

"Okay, well, I'm Sofiya, one of Molly's coworkers at the library here. It's a pleasure to meet both of you. I've heard good things, too."

"Her *coworker*," Naomi repeated with a glint in her eye that told Sofiya she was definitely missing something. She had the sense that she was being tested, but couldn't quite put her finger on what she was being tested for. Now she just had to hope she could pass it.

"Well, I think we could also be called friends, but we also work together, so... Yeah. Coworkers is the easiest term for it."

Naomi didn't answer, only took a bite of the powdered sugar and cinnamon covered mound of puff pastry known as a montblanc in front of her and then moaned. Sofiya smiled, knowing the reason. Claudia was an exceptional chef. Even the grumpiest old men on the county board of supervisors couldn't resist being delighted by her puff pastry creations. It was probably the only reason they'd been able to stay open in their first year of business and beyond till now.

"If you like that, you ought to try her cinnamon buns," Sofiya told her, pointing to the large, sticky rolls on the other side of the plate. "The cream cheese icing is to die for."

Savannah took her at her word and sliced the bun into thirds without saying anything. Each of them took a piece and popped it into their mouths. Judging by the sounds they made immediately after, they all liked it. Molly's eyes fluttered closed and Sofiya had to stop herself from biting her lip. It was an incredibly attractive motion. She imagined the other things that would bring that much instant joy to the woman.

"So, Sofiya," Savannah started. "What brought you to Chatham?"

"Like, today, or in general?"

Savannah and Naomi traded glances, then shrugged in unison. Both it was, then. She took a deep breath and answered in the most succinct way possible.

"Well, I live just down the street and Claudia texted me asking me to come visit. In general, my parents moved here just after I finished high school. I moved to Richmond for college and graduate school, but my mom got sick and needed my help, so I came back... and well, here I am."

"I didn't know that, about your mom," Molly said softly. "I'm sorry."

"Thank you," Sofiya murmured with a sad smile. "It's been a long time. Now what about y'all?"

"Oh, we're only here for the day," Naomi said. "Molly got her first real couch for Christmas from her folks and we were conscripted to help with set up and finally decorating her apartment."

"Oh my god, you make it sound like I hadn't unpacked any of my things. It wasn't that bad," Molly explained with a laugh. "Almost everything I had to put up was art or tapestries. All things that needed to be oriented carefully where they would be seen from the couch!"

"And what about those two boxes of books we found hidden in among them?" Savannah asked, a thin eyebrow arched playfully.

"Or the entire tub of clothing?" Naomi added cheekily.

"Okay, those were summer clothes. Who needs shorts and crop tops when it hasn't gotten above 40 degrees in two months?" Molly's voice squeaked and all Sofiya could do was smile. It was clear from the way they laughed at each other just how much the other women loved Molly and how much she loved them. It was good to see. And despite the age difference of more than a decade, she liked these women herself. Given enough time, she thought, they might grow to like her, too.

JANUARY 2

MOLLY

The library director had asked the entire staff to come in an hour early on the first Monday after New Year's. Molly couldn't help but wonder what it was going to cover. These meetings weren't uncommon, but Sarita had never made them mandatory in the six months Molly had been attending them. This one was.

Sarita stood by the conference room door, welcoming everyone in with a cheerful smile on her face. She was putting in an effort to be cheerful, but what Molly saw when she looked closely worried her. The deep bronze color of her normally glowing skin was much darker under the eyes and the wrinkle that had been there before the break was back with a vengeance. It left Molly with a pit in the bottom of her stomach that not even the delicious local pastries on the table would fill.

Slowly but surely, the rest of the staff filled the room. By the time the meeting was set to start, people were still wandering around saying good morning and she had anxiously picked apart a chocolate cinnamon swirl babka so that it was in bite sized pieces.

"Mind if I sit here?" The voice surprised her. She turned to find herself face to face with Sofiya, who looked radiant in a shimmery golden blouse and black blazer. When their eyes met, Sofiya smiled and suddenly the worry in her gut was a little bit more manageable. She smiled back and patted the chair.

"Of course not! Make yourself comfortable."

Molly waited for her to seat herself, then took her first bite of the babka. It was delicious. Isabelle took the seat on the other side of Sofiya, and their other coworkers from the various county branches filled in the rest of the conference table.

"Thank you for joining us, folks. I know it's early but I really appreciate you all being here this morning. Please, grab a snack and a cup of coffee if you haven't already."

Several of them reached for the pastries, but most of them had already grabbed what they wanted from the offerings. Sarita took a deep breath before continuing.

"First off, I'd like to thank all of you for your help in putting together the budget for your departments. As always, you are all awesome at your jobs. As you all know, it's budget season here in Chatham, which means that we have to present justification for just about every penny we want for next year's funding. However, if you've been reading the news lately, you'll also know that the county is tightening their belt for the third year in a row."

Everyone in the room groaned, Molly included. Every time the county "tightened their belts," it meant significantly less money came into the library system, which meant that it was even harder to provide for the residents who used the library on a daily basis.

"What's the word from the administration?" Isabelle asked worriedly. "How much does she think the board is going to take from us this year?"

"As always, the county administrator can't make any promises about what the board will do, but she says she won't be letting them cut more than ten percent from any of them."

The worry swirling in Molly's gut solidified into a real lump as the other librarians burst into whispers around the table. Ten percent of the library's budget was more than the cost of her salary and all the children's programming put together, and she was the most recently hired librarian. Would they fire her simply because of budget cuts? She knew it had happened to other librarians before.

Just the thought of going back on the job market already made her break into a cold sweat. When she thought about repacking all the things she had just finally gotten into a semblance of order, she wanted to cry. Before she could, though, she felt the lightest touch of a hand on her knee and the whisper of Sofiya's voice.

"We don't fire people for budget reasons. We cut down on the books we purchase, we cut down on programming, we hunt down grant funding for things we can't manage on our own. We might hold off on hiring new people, but you're in this with us, understand?"

She nodded, really holding back her tears now. She didn't know how Sofiya had known what she needed to hear, but she was glad that she had said it. Shortly afterwards, Sarita took over the meeting again and reiterated what the reference librarian had said.

"Now, all of your jobs are safe. That is just not how we work here in Pittsylvania County, but we are likely going to need to cut back on a lot of things. It's going to be rough, but we are going to make it through this as a team. Obviously, we won't know how much we'll have to cut back on as much as we can until discussions start next month to see if we can convince them that we're being good stewards of the funds they have given us. Does anyone have any questions?"

Breathing in deeply, she let a sigh pass through her glossy lips. It wasn't like they didn't already prove that they could work on a shoestring budget every day. The library system ran six fully-staffed libraries and a bookmobile throughout the areas they couldn't otherwise reach, helping to teach kids and adults alike the importance of literacy in all its forms. They were one of the only public places that could guarantee an internet connection six days a week that would also work through digital problems with anyone who needed it.

"Now, transitioning to the good news, there actually is good news!" Sarita grinned and the whole room laughed. "Library usage in general was up an average of nine percent from last year, which means that we've really been reaching the residents of the county. We had a three percent increase in our book checkout rate, a seventeen percent increase in program attendance, and a seven percent increase in technology assistance requests. Let's give a big round of applause to our social media team for that huge jump in attendance and for all of our hard work over the last year."

They all smiled at each other while applauding the increase. That was a great sign, a *provable* sign that what they were all spending their life doing mattered.

"That's all I've got for you at this meeting and it's almost time for those of us working today to get started, so keep up the good work, folks! And remember, we've still got time to lobby for more funding over the next three months. If you have any bright ideas, don't be afraid to share them with the rest of us!"

With that, the meeting was over. Molly still felt like the rug had been pulled out from underneath her, but she worked to compartmentalize it for later. She had to put on her best customer service persona and make every kid's experience with her programming the best it could be.

"Hey," a voice came from behind her again. This time she knew it was Sofiya before she turned. The older woman tucked a piece of hair behind her ear and smiled shyly. "Um, I know that all of that was a lot to process, but I was wondering if you were going to go to Rosebud's tonight for the New Year's party?"

"Honestly, I'd forgotten about it," she admitted. Sofiya's face fell a little before Molly continued. "But you know what? It sounds like a great party. I don't see why not!"

Sofiya smiled again and it made Molly's heart skip a beat. God, she was beautiful.

"I'm planning to get there around eight, so if we're there at the same time, I'd like to buy you a drink. Um, if that's not weird?"

Molly recognized Sofiya's motions as typical flirting, but wasn't sure how to process it. Was she actually flirting with her? On purpose? Or was she just being friendly and offering to buy a young coworker a drink after a stressful day? Or was Molly just projecting her own feelings onto the woman she'd been obsessing over? God, why did being gay have to make every single interaction with other women so much harder to figure out? If she wasn't flirting, then at least Molly could have a drink out of it and talk to a woman she considered a friend.

"I think I'd like that," she said shyly. "I will see you a little after eight, Sofiya."

Pleasure washed over the other woman's face and over Molly. Maybe it was flirting after all. She'd have to go the gay club if she wanted to find out for sure.

"I'll see you tonight then and leave you be for now. Have a good day!" And off the older woman went to the reference desk, a spring in her step that hadn't been there before. Now that she had something to look forward to, it would be a much better day than it had already set out to be.

SOFIYA

By the time Sofiya arrived at Rosebud, she had lost all of the boldness that had allowed her to tell Molly she wanted to buy her a drink, and that had allowed her to dress a little bit younger than usual. Pop music was blasting from the Greensboro bar, but her dancing spirit had positively fled. But, if she drove home now, she would have wasted two hours *and* she wouldn't get to see Molly in whatever her club outfit was. That would be the true travesty, especially after having seen her in her workout clothes.

Curiosity, and not wanting to stand the other woman up, was what brought Sofiya into the bar that night.

She took a few steps into the bar and looked around. What she saw when she entered took her breath away. The mahogany bar was covered in twinkle lights and tinsel in honor of the season, and LED fireworks had been placed on every free brick wall, making the room feel festive but not overly bright. The dance floor was already packed, despite it being relatively early for a party, and everyone seemed to be having a great time.

At the bar sat five people, two of whom Sofiya would have recognized from any angle - Claudia, in a black romper that hugged their body, and Molly, in the same blazer she'd worn to work. When she spun on her bar stool so that the light shone on her front, she could see that Molly had traded her work-appropriate gray wrap dress for a denim mini-skirt, patterned leggings and a shirt that stopped her heart.

Under the blazer, the light reflected off a shirt that was

more a leather harness than a garment. A collar with an O-ring connected strips of saddle-tanned orange leather that crisscrossed her chest. The bottom of the pentagram pattern connected to a slightly thicker band that sat right under her chest. Underneath it was a lacy black bralette that covered just enough to be vaguely appropriate and not an inch more. God, she was glad she'd come inside.

Her own shimmery silver button down was not quite as jaw-dropping, but it caught Molly's attention well enough. Sofiya watched as she elbowed Claudia and then both of them waved furiously at her. She waved back to acknowledge them and then, slowly, made her way over to them.

Claudia was the first to envelop her in a hug, but as soon as she was free, Sofiya couldn't take her eyes off the woman beside them. Molly reached out a hand and squeezed both of Sofiya's and a spark of electricity coursed through her. The hand squeeze then turned into a hug. Sofiya wanted to stay in that moment forever.

"Well, now that y'all have found each other, I'll leave you to it. Molly, if you find yourself in the mood for a dance, you can find me out there." They waved to the writhing mass of people dancing to a club remix of Janelle Monáe's Pink. "That is, if Sofiya doesn't sweep you off your feet first."

With a wink, they danced away. Sofiya blushed, but Molly was too preoccupied with watching them go. Her friend really was too much occasionally, but their final comment was the perfect chance for her to segue into the promised portion of the evening.

"Well, I don't know about sweeping you off your feet, but I'd love to buy you a drink. How does that sound?"

MOLLY

Molly bit down on the inside of her lip at the question in an attempt to avoid shouting her answer over the music and crowd. She had thought it might be a little overwhelming, but the music was great to have in the background after a day working with children who hadn't quite learned that whispering meant actually being quiet, not just making their voice raspy. It almost made it easier for her to focus on the person she'd come here to see.

And God, it was impossible not to focus on her. The twinkle lights all around the bar had enhanced the shimmer of Sofiya's silk blouse. It was one of the pieces she wore to work regularly, though she'd swapped out the trouser pants for skinny dark denim. On her, it was a look that turned Molly on more than she could put into words.

When Claudia had made their way into the crowd, Molly turned back around to see a stricken look on Sofiya's face. She had never actually answered her question.

"Sorry! Yes, absolutely. I'd love to have a drink with you." She gestured to the seats she and Claudia had occupied until Sofiya had arrived. The other woman slid into the formerly-empty stool beside her as Molly pulled herself into her own. She had to wiggle a little to make sure that the bulk of her weight was balanced on the thin backless stool, but Sofiya didn't seem to have any issue with it.

Before they could say anything else, the bartender sidled up. She was a very butch woman with short mauve hair that Molly would have been incredibly attracted to, if it hadn't been for the woman sitting next to her.

"What are we drinking, ladies?"

"I'll have a glass of the best white wine you've got," Sofiya requested before rummaging in her wallet for her credit card. "I'm buying for us both."

"Oh, um, I've never been here before. Do you have a cocktail menu?" Her question was met with a blank look and the bar equivalent of silence. Molly flushed, a little embarrassed at the confused stare the bartender was giving her. "Right. Um. I like gin, so how about you surprise me with your favorite drink to make?"

That brought a smile to the bartender's face before she took Sofiya's card, which made her feel a little bit better. Sofiya leaned forward on her stool and braced herself on the bar.

"You don't have a favorite cocktail? That surprises me."

Molly shrugged. "I don't really drink much. When I do, it's usually with Savannah and Naomi at home, so they usually make the decisions."

"Well, asking the bartender to make her favorite thing is a surefire way to get a good quality drink, even if it's not your personal favorite. And good alcohol is a surefire way to make a bad day a little bit easier to bear."

That turned Molly's smile into a grimace. She'd managed to put the funding problem out of her mind, at least enough to get herself ready to come to this place tonight.

She hadn't been to Rosebuds before and she hadn't been sure of the dress code, but she was glad she had chosen to go sexier than usual. The look on Sofiya's face when she had seen the harness had been worth every second of the cold she'd dealt with on the way in tonight. But that wasn't what she needed to be focusing on right now, even if it had been incredibly affirming.

"Today was rough, that's for sure. Is them 'tightening their belts' and cutting a huge portion of their operating budget kind of standard?"

Sofiya made a weighing motion with her hands and shrugged. "The county is super Republican, so the leadership has never really bothered gathering enough income to make the county livable. Hell, it took them this long to be willing to put even the least amount of money towards getting decent internet *for themselves*. The last few years, though... the Cheeto has inspired them to try to cut taxes more while the rest of us run on fumes."

"Of course he did." Molly rolled her eyes. "Bastard."

"I'll drink to that," the bartender laughed, startling Molly a little bit. She had two drinks in her hand, one a glass of white wine and one a bright pink drink with several ice cubes and pineapple and cherry on the rim. Molly didn't recognize it, but assumed it was for her.

"All right, ma'am, tonight I have made a Singapore Sling, which features cherry brandy, Benedictine, pineapple and lime juice, and of course, gin. Let me know if you don't like it or if you need anything else."

Molly thanked her while she wrapped her hands around the drink. It was cold and smelled sweet, but not overpoweringly so. Sofiya sipped at her wine while Molly took a sip of her own drink. It was delightful! She told the bartender so, earning a grin and a small bow before making her way down towards some women that were calling her name further down the bar, leaving Molly and Sofiya effectively alone with their drinks.

"So what does the budget process look like?" Molly asked. "I've never been through one before."

"Before they make a decision, Sarita, and probably some of the staff will have several chances to speak to the board privately about why we need the funding. That usually causes them to reel back the proposed changes a little bit. After that, there's a couple of public hearings over the next few months. They're open to the public, but almost no one shows up to speak about the changes, and then one final vote in public in May where everyone shows up to bitch about the things they previously said nothing about."

"Well, at least there's a chance for us to fight back against this bullshit," Molly grumbled. "Maybe we can get all of the librarians and some of the patrons involved to help us out."

"It has helped before," Sofiya agreed. "It certainly can't hurt to show them how much everything in our library gets used. I mean, even the video equipment we offer gets used so regularly that we've had to purchase another set."

Molly sat straighter at the mention of the video equipment. She knew the set Sofiya meant - a Canon DSLR camera body, two fixed-length lenses a tripod and an attachable light. It was the perfect set for small films and even pretty decent photography.

"We're getting another camera set?" That could be useful. The current set was pretty much constantly checked out by high schoolers and community college students,

"I think that gets delivered next week, which is not ideal for this austere budget we're going to have to pretend we can function under, but we bought it six months ago."

Sofiya grimaced but Molly was too busy thinking about ways that she could make sure their voices were heard. That applied in more ways than one, as the DJ came over the speaker system much louder than usual. She leaned closer to Sofiya, wheels turning while she thought out loud.

"I'm just spit balling, so I don't know if this is allowed, but what if we made a video to show the board exactly what people are most grateful for at the library? To show why it's meaningful for the community?"

Sofiya froze, her nearly empty wine glass halfway to her lightly glossed lips.

"Sorry, you can tell me if that's ridiculous. It was just a half-formed thought." Molly fiddled with her cocktail napkin, suddenly a little embarrassed, when Sofiya set her glass down hard on top of the bar.

"No, no! It's a great idea! I just wish we'd thought of it before. We could even send it to Fiona at the local paper. Hell, maybe we'd get some TV coverage, too. After all, this is the digital era and our social media team has been getting some great results…"

Molly grinned, then caught the synthesized piano notes that were the introduction to the dance remix of Zedd and Foxes' *Clarity* - one of her favorites.

"Oh, I love this song!" Molly squealed suddenly. "My sister would kick my ass if I came all the way out here tonight looking this good and didn't dance with anyone. Sofiya, let's go dance!"

She didn't miss the way Sofiya's eyes followed the strips of leather to her bare navel and back up again before she answered her. She felt herself flushing, and was once again glad that no one would be able to tell in the bar's lighting.

"I would love to dance with you, Molly. We'll talk about the library later."

By the time the beat dropped, both Sofiya and Molly were dancing in time with the music, rocking back and forth without letting go of each other's hands. Molly couldn't remember the last time she'd had this much fun with anyone other than Savannah and Naomi. This night had turned out to be even more than she'd hoped for.

Molly felt herself gaining a clearer picture of what she wanted from her relationship with Sofiya with every beat of the remixed song. It wasn't perfectly clear yet, but it was a start. She wanted Sofiya in both a sexual and platonic way.

Now, she just had to figure out if Sofiya really wanted the same thing from her and how to make it work while working together. Easy as apple pie, right?

JANUARY

MOLLY

It took two and a half weeks for the camera equipment to be delivered, but that had been more than enough time for Molly to talk to Sarita and the IT director about what she needed to do to make sure all of her ducks were in a row for her project.

She had to agree to let the library use the footage in perpetuity, so there were some kinks to work out with the filming process. Legally, she needed to make sure that everyone whose face appeared even slightly in a piece of video signed a media release, and that all of those were digitized along with the footage. So, she had one of the releases and black pens in the hands of each parent in the audience and the tripod set up to get footage from the back of the kids' area. She was excited and ready for to start doing her best to help the library.

At least, until Andrew Scott walked up to her with the release in his large hands and an angry look on his face.

He stopped mere inches away from her, shaking the form at her.

"What the hell is this? Why do I need to sign a media release for my son to take part in story time?" He demanded.

Molly stood firm, even though he was so close she could smell his cologne. "Sir, please lower your voice. We are in a public library and there is no reason for you to be speaking like that to me."

She watched his nostrils flare before he took a deep breath to try and calm himself down.

"Why are we signing media releases today, Ms. Andersen? We've never needed to do that before."

"Well, like it says right there at the top of the page, we are starting on a new project to help show off everything that we do here at the library as part of our new, digital campaign and to present it to the board. Part of that is getting video of people enjoying things at the library, which is why we need a release form."

He took another deep breath, but let his shoulders slump as if he'd already been defeated. It was then she noticed the dark circles under his eyes.

"I... I can't sign this for him. Part of the settlement was that everything media-related had to go through my... It has to go through Tara's... Mayor Scott's office. You know how it is when you're a public figure."

Molly would hardly have called the mayor of a town of 1500 a public figure, but divorce settlements were divorce settlements. Besides, Molly had made a plan for that. She smiled at him and he took a step back, apparently realizing he was way too far into her space.

"Well, it sounds like you have two options. You can either call the mayor's office and get permission for a good cause or you can both sit off to either side of the camera so that you won't be on film." She pointed to the spaces she'd cleared out specifically for this reason.

His pale skin flushed when he saw the group of colorful cushions waiting for someone to sit on them. It was clear he hadn't noticed them before, just lost control of his emotions at the thought of calling his ex-wife for anything. That had to be painful.

"I'm so sorry, Ms. Anderson. I really don't mean to be an a... a jerk. We've had a rough week, but that's no excuse for me to take it out on you."

She had to smile at the amendment to his apology. He had been working harder at being a good parent to his son, and she had been enjoying seeing them grow closer over the last few weeks. It had been almost enough for her to forgive him for asking her out, and definitely enough for her to see that there was a decent enough person in there.

"You're right, that isn't an excuse. But I appreciate the apology all the same. Are you doing all right? You seem down today."

"I'm a parent. I don't get to not be okay." He shrugged and laughed harshly. "No matter what's going on with his mother, *I* have to be okay for him."

"Wow. It sounds like you could use a break."

"Desperately, but it's story time and then I have to go back to work while he naps, so I don't get one today."

He scrubbed a hand over his eyes that might have been wiping away a few tears. It softened her heart just a little. She looked around the room and counted the number of adults available. There were several people wearing volunteer badges milling around the room looking lost. It gave Molly an idea.

"Look, we've got some extra volunteers today. I don't usually offer this, but... do you want to leave Matt with us for story time so you can go get some coffee from The Crescent or something?"

"Are you sure?" His eyes filled with tears and he didn't bother trying to hide it. She nodded and he wiped them away again.

"Go. We'll keep him out of view of the cameras. Come back in half an hour and he'll be ready for you. Tell Claudia you came from the library and you'll get a discount."

She beckoned over one of the older volunteers, who waited patiently while Andrew wrote out a note with his information on it, just in case, and explained what was happening to his son. He watched as the volunteer led the three-year-old to the cushions and sat, talking about something she couldn't hear.

"Thank you, Molly. I owe you one." And with that, he almost sprinted out the door. Maybe someday she'd use that owed favor to her advantage. For now, though, she had a room full of kids to read to, and a video to start recording. She watched another volunteer press the record button at her signal, and breathed a sigh of relief when the little red light glowed in the corner.

"All right, kids! Who's ready to read *Dragons Love Tacos*?"

SOFIYA

A few days after the camera arrived, Sofiya had been in charge of opening the library and thus, was the first one there. She loved a silent library almost as much as she loved one that was jam-packed full of patrons. It was the perfect time to put together the monthly reports that always came due at the end of the month before any of her coworkers needed anything from her.

The first coworker in that morning was, of course, Molly. Sofiya looked up at the sound of the door opening, just in time to see her make an entrance by tripping over the threshold and falling face first while trying to push her way in the library's second set of doors with a few too many bags in hand. Sofiya rushed to her from around the circulation desk to help her up and found the young librarian on her

"Oh, goodness! Are you okay?"

"I'm all right." Molly laughed and shook her head. "This is what I get for trying to get everything in from my car in one trip,"

Offering her a hand, Sofiya helped Molly get to her feet. The bags she had carried were scattered around her.

"What is all of this anyway?" Sofiya asked bemusedly. "The camera equipment you checked out only takes up two bags and you have... five, including your purse."

Once she'd dusted herself off, Molly pointed to each of the bags in turn. "Those two are ours, that one is a microphone set up I borrowed from a friend, and that one is my laptop for easy uploading during the day. Oh, and I brought in some donation books that someone handed me. Those are in my purse."

"Why do you need a microphone? I thought there was one in the camera?"

"Well, yeah but I didn't like the way the sound echoed when I tried to do interviews, and those are an important part of my project. Iveta, the new PR girl at DCC had one that wasn't being used, so she loaned it to me."

"Oh, I didn't know you knew Iveta! That was very cool of her. Let me help you carry some of these in so you don't fall again."

"Thanks, that would be great."

Molly beamed, then bent down to pick up a bag. Sofiya bent at almost the same moment and reached for one of the black camera bags, only to find her fingers colliding and intertwining with Molly's instead. Sofiya's heart raced at the touch but she didn't pull away. Neither, she noticed, did Molly. Slowly, their eyes met over the bag and Sofiya felt her cheeks flush like she was a schoolgirl again.

A cold blast of winter wind rushed through the library doors as they opened and the two women sprang apart like they'd been caught doing something much more intimate than holding hands and gazing into each other's eyes.

"Good morning, ladies. Everything all right here?" Sarita looked down at them where they crouched on the floor with both of her thick black eyebrows raised. Sofiya's flush deepened but when she tried to answer, Molly answered for her.

"I tripped on my way in and dropped all of my stuff. Sofiya was just helping me carry it in."

Sarita nodded and stepped around them. Before she walked through the other set of doors, she turned back to them.

"Oh, Sofiya, I meant to tell you, the meeting you were supposed to host got canceled, so you're going to have a light day today."

Sofiya straightened at that. She hadn't had a light day since before the holiday season between setting up final study programs for the students, making sure everyone had their budget forms in, and preparing her panel proposal for the regional librarian conference. Her proposal on digital archiving had been declined because it was too similar to another panel they had already planned, but that was the way of things with conferences.

Unfortunately, that meant most of her day would get filled at the circulation desk. Unless... She glanced sidelong at Molly, who had grabbed the two camera bags and stood.

"Hey, Molly - did you want some help filming today?"

Molly's eyes lit up. Before she could answer, Sarita clapped her hands. "Oh, that's a great idea, Sofiya! I'm sure Molly would love your help! I've seen what she's filmed so far and it's wonderful. I bet between the two of you, you'll be able to get even better video. Perfect."

Without waiting for an answer, their boss pushed through the doors and bustled into their library.

"It would definitely make editing easier if someone managed the camera during the interviews," Molly admitted with an impish smile that hid *some* of her wicked thoughts. "How good are you at following directions, Sofiya? I'm very bossy."

Sofiya's heart fluttered in her chest as her smile curved to match the younger woman's. She picked up the remaining bags and stood.

"Oh, I think I can handle you." It came out flirtier than she had intended it, but Molly looked her up and down with delight written on her face.

"We'll see about that, won't we?"

MOLLY

The following week followed basically the same pattern every day. Whenever Molly and Sofiya had a few moments where they weren't actively needed for programming or to work the front desk, they were asking patrons what they used the library for most, and why it was valuable to them.

At first, it was difficult to find people who were willing to be filmed, but as they did more interviews, people learned what they were working on. After a few days, people started to come prepared with nicer clothes and enough makeup to make them comfortable in front of the camera.

By the time Friday rolled around, there were people lined up around the room to wait to be interviewed for the project when Molly walked in from her lunch break. The corner that they had turned into a filming space was occupied by a trio of familiar people. Andrew stood behind the wingback chair where Matt sat cross-legged with a grin like the sun. Sofiya stood behind the camera with a look of focus on her face. She didn't look back when Molly walked up.

"And... go. Matt, say your name and how old you are, please."

"My name's Matt and I'm three!" He held up three fingers on one hand and looked at his dad.

"And I'm Andrew Scott, his dad. We visit the Pittsylvania County library three times a week for story time with Ms. Andersen and we are so grateful for all of the services that they provide for everyone in our community. Libraries are vital for growing a community and we hope ours will continue to grow as much as possible in the next few years."

Three seconds later, Sofiya had ended the recording and finally looked at Molly. Sweat had beaded around her eyes where she'd had her face pressed to the camera. Molly's fingers itched to wipe it away and move the bangs from her eyes. Instead, she intertwined her fingers in front of her.

"I had to get started without you, sorry. We've had quite a few volunteers for our video project." That was an understatement. Molly couldn't believe it. There had to be thirty people lined up of all ages and races. It was honestly astounding.

"No kidding. Do you have releases for everybody already?" Sofiya shook her head. "Then I'll start doing that while you keep filming. This ought to net us more than enough footage to finish."

"Sounds good. Mrs. Scearce? Come on up!"

She dug the forms out of the bag at Sofiya's feet and without further discussion, she got to work.

SOFIYA

By the end of the day, Sofiya was dead on her feet. She didn't think she had sat down for more than a few minutes all afternoon. Had she known that was what her day would hold, she would have worn more comfortable shoes. She wouldn't have stayed home for anything, though. Seeing the delight on Molly's face while they filmed and knowing that it was going to be a fantastic video had made every minute worth it. They still needed to edit the video into one piece, but that was a problem for later.

Right now, her only plan was to go home to snuggle on the

couch with her cat and a glass of wine until Claudia closed up the cafe and arrived with takeout from the new Mediterranean restaurant in town. It was the perfect plan and Luke was more than happy to help her stick to it.

The instant she slid her flats off, the gray cat was rolling all over them with gusto while she petted him with her bare foot. When she made her way into her bedroom, he followed, chirping while she changed into her favorite flowing cotton maxi dress. It had been black when she bought it, but thanks to the cat fur that had become ingrained in the fabric, it was now mostly gray. She was glad that no one but Claudia saw her in it because they would think she was the perfect image of the stereotypical single lesbian cat lady. Which she was, of course, but she didn't want the rest of the town to know that.

Dating options had been slim in Chatham for a long time, thanks to the area being incredibly Republican and old-fashioned, but that had been okay with Sofiya. She had never been the kind of woman to need to be in a relationship all the time to be happy. Claudia and her friends from the library, as well as a few relationships, had been great company for years.

Lately, though, she had caught herself wishing there was someone for her to come home to and share her life with, someone to snuggle up with other than the cat. She wasn't sure exactly when it had started to change, but those daydreams of having a partner in life had become more and more common over the last few weeks. As she poured herself a glass of red wine, she couldn't help but wonder what Molly was doing at that moment. Was she walking to her own couch to watch something on Netflix? Or was she out getting dinner and drinks with another of the younger queer folks in the area? Was she hitting it off with someone new?

That last thought brought a stab of something like jealousy as she settled herself into the corner of the couch and stretched her legs across the cushions. She hated that she was jealous of something that probably wasn't even happening and that she couldn't bring herself to say something to Molly about how she felt. If she did say something, she worried that Molly would be hurt or feel like she was trying to push a romantic relationship onto her. She really didn't want that to happen.

With a small prrt sound, Luke hopped up at her feet and then walked up her legs until he reached her lap. He shoved his head in her free hand and she laughed. It wasn't the first time she'd wished she could be more like her cat - unapologetic in asking for exactly what he needed, whether it was food or attention. She didn't want all the fur, though. She had enough hair to deal with as it was.

Unlocking her phone, she turned on her audiobook to where she'd left off and let the narrator's voice wash over her while she petted the beast on her lap. For right now, this was all she needed. She would figure out the rest later.

∼

MOLLY

Once the video was done being filmed, Molly had been given permission to stay after hours in the IT cubicle and work on editing it into hours. She soon realized that editing video was nowhere near as glamorous as the movies made it out to be. Throughout the day, she had been coming back and uploading more videos from the various memory cards they'd used so everything had been uploaded, but nothing was labeled and she hadn't scanned any of the release forms yet. It was going to take *forever*.

Just looking at the piles and the digital folders and knowing she had to do all of the work on her own made her want to scream. Before she could, the door opened and Sofiya's head popped in. Molly almost laughed. It was like the other woman had an otherworldly sense for other people's unhappy emotions and she had to come and fix them as soon as humanly possible.

"Oh, hey! I didn't know you were back here." Sofiya's voice was light and cheerful despite having had a busy day full of meetings. "Have you seen Isabelle? I needed to ask her something about the new software."

"She left early - one of her kids had a doctor's appointment, I think. I just took over her office to work on the video."

"Oh well. I'll just talk to her about it whenever she's back. It's nothing major." She shrugged, but lingered in the doorway. "You're working on editing tonight?"

"Not quite," Molly grimaced. "I think I'm going to spend the evening scanning these releases and organizing all of the files. I might get to editing tomorrow if I'm lucky."

Sofiya's eyes traveled the room, taking in all the camera equipment, piles of paperwork and finally, Molly's expression. She could feel the woman's gaze on the sweat that beaded above her pinched lips and the way her hands rubbed the back of her neck. She was the picture of agitation.

"Sarita mentioned you were staying late tonight..." She bit her lip and Molly could tell she was thinking hard. "Do you want some help? I'm not quite as savvy as you with the technology, but-"

"Please!" Molly cut her off with an excited yelp that she tried to cover with shaking hands. When she thought she had herself under control, she tried speaking again. "You don't even have to do anything, just the company would be so nice to have."

Sofiya snorted. "Like I'm going to sit here and do nothing while you work your ass off sorting all kinds of things. No. What I will do is go grab dinner for us both while you get yourself situated. What are you in the mood for - pizza, Mexican or Claudia's?"

"Ooh, Mexican food sounds good." The idea of a mass of carbs and cheese and spices made her mouth water. She gave Sofiya her order - arroz con pollo with choriqueso - and plugged in her headphones so she could get started with the labeling. Sofiya's hand fell on her shoulder and squeezed gently. She looked up at the older woman and found her standing there with an unreadable yet soft expression on her face. Before Molly could ask, Sofiya's hand fell away and she slipped out of the room. Molly watched her go and pressed her own hand to where Sofiya's had been moments before, waiting for her heart to stop racing.

SOFIYA

Sofiya could have kicked herself all the way to the restaurant. Just squeezing her shoulder and then running away? It was cowardly and ridiculous, especially since Molly had never given her permission to be touched. She hadn't gotten a good look at her face before she'd fled and she found herself praying while she waited for their food that the other woman wouldn't think that it was harassment. Even if she knew that it was what she deserved, after months of lusting after her from across the sea of books and patrons.

While she walked back to the library with the food, she thought about all the ways that she could apologize for the action without making the rest of the evening awkward. She could say it as soon as she got back, simply let it burst from her chest the way it wanted to, but there was no way that wouldn't be weird. It was also possible to just work it into the conversation they were sure to have later in the evening, but then it would sound like she'd spent the whole night thinking about it, which would make it even weirder. Every option she came up with had its own problems.

By the time she locked the library doors behind herself, she decided that she just wouldn't say anything unless Molly did. When she walked into the IT office, Molly still had her headphones in. Sofiya waved with her free hand to try and get her attention, but Molly continued staring at the screen in front of her. She called her name and still got no response. Carefully, she set the bag of food down next to the other computer in the room. Molly still did not react. She had to let her know that she was there, but once again, the best way to communicate with her was by touch.

Gently, she tapped the Black woman on the shoulder then instantly reeled back. Molly whipped around with a shriek, her braids hitting Sofiya's hands with all the force physics would grant them.

"Sorry! Sorry! It's me!" Sofiya cried out. After a moment, Molly recognized her and closed her eyes. She took a deep shuddering breath before she opened them again.

"*God*, you scared me, Sof! Can't you give a girl a little warning?"

"I tried!" Sofiya burst into laughter and Molly joined in a few seconds later. "Man, it's a really good thing I'm not a robber. You'd have been in deep shit if I was."

"Pfft. I can take care of myself. Besides, who robs a county library? We have almost nothing worth reselling that most people know about. You'd get a better haul out of any house on Main Street. Plus, you locked the door behind you when you left. I heard it."

Oh, so she'd heard *that*. Sofiya had to admit she had a point, but still. "I'm sorry that I scared you. And that I touched you without permission twice? I should have asked first."

Molly smiled at her and most of her anxiety ebbed away. "I didn't mind the touch the first time. That second one, though, that I was not expecting at all!"

They both laughed again.

"Anyway, the food is here so you should eat before you dig in again. I'll do the same, then get started on scanning these releases for you."

The look of gratitude on Molly's face warmed Sofiya from nose to toes as she dug into her own food with gusto. For several minutes, there was very little sound between them other than that of their meals, and one request to pass a napkin across the mere foot of space that separated their desks.

When they were finished, they both went back to their tasks in continued comfortable silence. Sofiya was amazed how easily the time passed when they were together despite the tedious task at hand. It had been years since she had felt this comfortable in someone other than Claudia's presence, and longer than that since she'd found herself looking for any excuse to spend time with someone. She adored Molly - the way she threw herself into everything she did, the way she styled herself, hell, even the way she acted with her sister and best friend. She couldn't help but seek out ways to spend time with her and learn more and more about her because every new thing she discovered, she liked even more.

After a while, Sofiya felt a tap on her shoulder. Just like Molly had earlier, she jumped. She had no idea how long she'd been at her task, but the pile was dwindling. Molly had unplugged her headphones and was looking at her expectantly.

"Come over here. You've got to see this video. This kid is *so* cute!"

Sofiya stood up and stretched her back, feeling the

tendons in her lower back stretch and pop. They really needed to get more comfortable chairs back here. She didn't know how Isabelle sat in them all day long. Making her way over to Molly's side, she leaned down until her face was level with the other librarian's. She couldn't help but notice just how close they were, how Molly's breath fluttered with residual laughter and how she smelled like cocoa butter and ginger.

She breathed the scent of her in before she spoke. "Ready when you are!"

Molly clicked the mouse and a recording of an elementary aged girl in a Minnie Mouse-esque dress seated in the very front of the chair she was in. Sofiya was already smiling before she started speaking with the inevitable lisp of a child missing their front teeth.

"Mommy takes me to the library every day so that I can check out more boobs!" A woman who was probably her mother rushed onto the screen with a stricken expression.

"Books! She means books!"

The girl squinted at her mother with all the righteous indignation a six-year-old could muster. "That's what I said. Boobs!"

Both of them burst into laughter as they exchanged glances. As she leaned forward with glee, Sofiya noticed for the first time the flecks of hazel and green in Molly's eyes as they crinkled with laughter. When Molly's forehead fell to Sofiya's shoulder, the older woman froze. Her scent was overwhelming all of her other senses except for the feeling of her heart fluttering. She hadn't known that this small contact could feel so perfect.

Molly lifted her head so that her brown eyes met Sofiya's with a question written plainly in them. The way her gaze darted from Sofiya's lips and back up to her eyes brought a surge of longing coursing through Sofiya's body. Before she could stop herself, she leaned in and pressed her lips to Molly's. She was gentle at first, wanting to make it easy for Molly to pull away if she had read her signals all wrong, then deeper as she felt the other woman melt into her touch.

She felt Molly suck gently on her lower lip and couldn't stop herself from moaning into her mouth. She knew this was wrong, that they were at work and it would make everything complicated, but it felt *so* right. If Sofiya had opened her eyes, she would have seen the flush on Molly's face, but she couldn't bring herself to possibly ruin this beautiful, perfect moment. When Molly wrapped her hand around the back of Sofiya's neck, she was lost in the moment.

That hand on her neck was the only thing that kept her from falling flat on her ass when a banging sound echoed through the library. The shock sent them both reeling. The movement was so sharp that Molly's phone clattered to the ground in an echo of the metallic banging that was coming from the front of the library. Sofiya stared at the empty space where she had just been with confusion. What on earth was happening?

The only thing that could make that sound would be the front door, but they had been closed for several hours now. Who could possibly be banging on it as if their life depended on it?

"What the hell?" Molly mumbled, her hand pressed to

her lips. "Why is someone banging on the door? We're closed."

Sofiya waited to see if the sound would stop while she tried to process what she had just done - what *they* had just done. But the banging continued until neither of them could stand the sound. Molly still hadn't moved from the chair and she couldn't tell what the shock on her face was from, or whether it was good or bad.

"I'll go see what it is," Sofiya grumbled. She made her way through the hallway and around the circulation desk. The noise in the entryway was unbearable after the soft quiet of the back office. Standing in front of the glass doors was a large, older man that bundled up in so many layers of warm clothes that she almost couldn't tell who he was. When she got right up to the doors, though, she did recognize him as a regular patron. He held up two books and she groaned.

"Sir, we are closed." She emphasized her point by literally pointing to the closed sign. He simply shook the books at her and continued knocking on the door until she opened it.

"We have been closed for more than two hours. You'll have to return your books using our after-hours drop off."

"But you're still here! Can't you just check them in real fast, Ms. Anderson?" His face was pleading underneath his hat, but it wasn't working on her. Much cuter patrons had tried to get her to do favors in her time and she had not

"No, Mr. Warren, I cannot. We have a policy for a reason.

Anything left after the doors close will be checked in the following morning."

He puffed up at her words, clearly offended despite her entirely civil tone.

"Well, I never! You're still here so you ought to check my books in. That's what libraries are for, you uppity little -"

"*Mister* Warren," she cut him off using her well-practiced severe librarian voice. It worked to stop him from using whatever expletive was about to come out of his mouth. "You have been a patron here longer than I've been a librarian. You ought to know better than to carry on like this. I cannot, and even if I could, I will not check your book in for you. Leave it in the drop box and we will get it in the morning."

His face hardened at her wintry voice, but she stood her ground until he grunted and walked away without another word. Sofiya waited until he got into his over-sized SUV and drove away before she went back inside. By the time she got back to the office, Molly had packed up her computer and had donned her own hat and coat. Sofiya's heart sank, knowing that the moment they'd shared before was now only in her memory.

"I'm done for the night. I'll... I'll see you in the morning." Molly's voice was quiet and emotionless.

"Do... did you not want to talk about...?" Sofiya didn't know what had happened in the minutes she'd been gone, but she'd assumed that they would talk about the kiss. Or maybe pick up where they'd left off?

"I just- I have to go," Molly stammered. Sofiya didn't try

to stop her, only stood there with her heart in the pit of her stomach while she brushed past her out the door. She could only hope she hadn't ruined things with a woman she now realized that she cared very deeply for.

MOLLY

Molly's palms were sweating like nobody's business. She couldn't believe how nervous she was about showing the video to Sarita. The library director had already seen most of the footage and had said how much she loved it. Besides, it wasn't like the video would do any harm if it wasn't absolutely perfect. The old men on the board knew she wasn't a professional videographer, but even so, she thought that she and Sofiya had done a fairly good job. Now, all she had left to do was wait. She was spending that time sweating, thinking and flicking the flash drive open and shut.

She hadn't anticipated just how much help Sofiya would be on the project. She also hadn't anticipated how much *fun* she would have working alongside the older woman. Over the last week, she had caught herself looking forward to spending the days filming with her and then that one evening cooped up in the tiny library office together. And then when the kiss had happened... well, that had been a nice surprise. Maybe, just maybe Sofiya had some kind of feelings towards her. I mean, that was what a kiss signaled for most alloromantic people, right?

As if she knew Molly was thinking about something non-work appropriate, Sofiya chose that moment to walk into the office with a smile on her face. They hadn't talked since the kiss and Molly had no idea how she was supposed to handle it. She'd run off at the first chance in an attempt to manage her own emotions, which was probably the wrong choice.

"Hey, you ready to do this?" Her voice was soft and kind. Almost on cue, Molly flicked the flash drive a little too hard and it slipped from her sweaty hand. Before she could react, Sofiya had reached a hand out and caught the black and orange device that held everything they'd worked on for weeks. "Are you all right?"

She pressed the drive into Molly's palm and folded her fingers over it so gently that Molly thought she might cry. She wasn't sure why, but something about the tenderness in Sofiya's eyes touched her much more deeply than the whisper of her fingers. Molly opened her mouth to say something, though she wasn't sure what, when Sarita walked in.

She looked at their hands and then up to each of their faces with raised eyebrows.

"This is the second time I have walked in on the two of you holding hands. Is there something you would like to tell me?"

Sofiya's cheeks turned bright pink as Molly tried to stammer out a reply. Luckily, the older woman hadn't lost control of her voice.

"No, Sarita. There's nothing to be said. Molly just dropped her flash drive."

Sarita pursed her lips thoughtfully for a moment as she

looked over their faces, but eventually, she nodded. Molly wasn't sure that their boss believed them, but honestly, she wasn't sure exactly what they would be able to tell her anyway.

"Well, I feel I should tell you that the county has begun changing its policies to disallow relationships between employees who work in the same department. Anyone who enters into such a relationship would need to talk to human resources to ensure the county is protected from any sexual harassment lawsuits. Do you understand?"

Both of the women nodded without looking at each other. Apparently satisfied, Sarita clapped her hands together and motioned for them to follow her into her office.

"Since there is nothing else to talk about, let's watch this video of yours."

Molly went into the room first, plugging the flash drive into the first available slot and waiting for it to pop up on the desktop. She couldn't help but be aware of how her body was pointed as she bent over the desk to open the file, knowing that Sofiya would have no choice but to staring at her ass because of how small the office was. Once the video player opened, Molly made her way to the chair next to Sofiya. Sarita pressed play for herself and waited.

The first image on the screen was footage of Molly reading to the toddlers with Sofiya's voice over it.

"Libraries are an important part of life for many members of the community, no matter how old they are. We talked to some of our patrons to see what they love most about the Pittsylvania County libraries."

Video after video of children, teenagers, parents and seniors played on the screen over some inoffensive classical music they had found on a stock site. Molly wasn't focused on it, though. She was too busy avoiding looking at where Sofiya's arm rubbed against hers on the arm rest between their chairs, and looking at her boss's face to see what she thought of the video.

Sarita smiled at some interviews and laughed at others, which Molly was pretty sure was a good sign. The interviews had turned out even more beautifully than she'd thought they would. Molly was so focused on everything else that she jumped at the sound of her own voice at the end of the video reminding people to make sure to support their local library. She could feel Sofiya smothering a laugh and she elbowed her gently with a playful scowl.

Sofiya just grinned at her, showing the deep laugh lines that Molly found so beautiful. She had to resist the urge to laugh herself when Sarita turned around.

"That... was wonderful!" She exclaimed. "I didn't expect anything near this level of quality from you two. This looks almost professional!"

Molly wasn't sure whether to be offended or pleased. Looking at Sofiya's face, she could tell the other woman felt the same way.

"I think we need to show this to the county administrator right away. It will do wonders to help get the board members to realize just how important all of our funding is to the community they claim to serve. This is just wonderful, ladies! I'm so pleased!"

Molly couldn't help but be thrilled. She glanced at Sofiya and saw pride written on her face.

"Thank you, Sarita. I had a great time working on it."

"We both did." Sofiya nodded and smiled at her. Molly's heart leaped a little in her chest like the traitorous organ it was. Hadn't they just been scolded for being too close at work? She couldn't afford to lose this job over something she couldn't even be sure she was feeling, something that she and Sofiya had never talked about.

"I'll show this to her and the social media team right away," Sarita continued. "You two can go back out onto the floor now."

Molly knew a dismissal when she heard it and so did Sofiya. They both turned towards the door, but stopped when Sarita spoke again.

"Oh, I forgot to mention this to you. The administration declined the funding request for mileage for two cars to go to Richmond."

"What?" Sofiya's head snapped up. "Why would they do that?"

"Apparently the board has decided that they won't pay for travel outside of the county borders." Sarita rolled her eyes.

"We got grant funding for literally everything else for the entire week, including the hotel room! Why... Never mind, I know why," Molly grumbled. "Penny pinching old men."

"And that worked in your favor, sort of. They were going

to decline to fund both cars, but I was able to talk them into allowing one because of how frugal you both had been with public funds. But, that means that you two are going to need to carpool to the conference next week."

Molly felt her eyes widen as she glanced at the other woman. This was going to be an *experience*.

FEBRUARY 12

SOFIYA

Sofiya wished that she could have gotten away with driving herself to the conference. She also wished that she hadn't asked Molly to come pick her up at her house. Sure, it made more sense for her to leave her truck at home instead of in Molly's driveway, but she was suddenly overcome with the desire to ensure that her home was cleaner than it had ever been before. What if Molly came inside and judged her for the clutter on her bathroom counters? Would the fine coating of dust on the windowsills horrify her? Was she allergic to cats?

Realistically, she probably wouldn't even come into the house. And even if she did, there was no way a 26-year-old who had just finished grad school had her life together enough to have her bathroom perfectly organized. Especially since she hadn't unpacked her decorations for six months after moving to town. Sofiya kept a clean house. No one other than a bloodhound would be able to smell the cat litter at all, the trash had been taken out, and the dishes had been washed.

Despite reminding herself of this repeatedly, Sofiya found herself dusting the window sills in her living room when Molly's new-looking turquoise Ford hatchback pulled into the driveway behind her own slightly rusted red pickup truck. She knew it looked —and was— silly, but she couldn't help but feel better about her house with just that tiny improvement.

By the time Molly knocked on the yellow front door, Sofiya had hidden the tools of her ridiculousness, wiped the dust off of her own clothing, and made sure she had all of her things. Her purse sat on top of her memory foam pillow which was strapped to the top of her rolling suitcase. It would be nearly impossible for her to forget all of it when it was essentially one unit.

When Sofiya answered the door, Molly stood there with her hands shoved into the front pockets of her distressed jeans and an easy smile on her face. She looked like she didn't have a care in the world and Sofiya couldn't help but smile back. The bright early afternoon sun shone down on her through the porch slats, leaving brush strokes of sunlight against the dark canvas of her skin. If she had been a photographer or painter with any skill, it would have been an award winning picture. They still hadn't talked about the kiss or anything like it, so Sofiya had avoided showing her attraction, but Sofiya hadn't stopped admiring her.

"Well, hey there. You ready to roll?"

"Give me just one minute to say goodbye to my furry beast. You're welcome to come in."

Molly stepped over the threshold and let the door close behind her. As if he'd been waiting for the click of the door, the short-haired gray cat in a lime green bow tie collar came running into the living room. He looked up at her with wide eyes that Sofiya knew matched his tie, as if he was horrified by her presence in his space.

"Molly, this is Luke. Luke, this is my friend Molly. You can say hi."

"Oh, hey, buddy!" Molly cooed, falling instantly into baby talk. She crouched and held out a hand to the concerned cat, only for him to head-butt it almost instantly. "Who's a handsome kitty? You are! Yes, you are!"

Sofiya shook her head at him while she tried to hide how quickly her heart was melting at the sight. Luke was a good judge of character, but it was rare for him to start chirping his purrs at someone he'd only sniffed once. It had taken him at least five minutes to be done sniffing Claudia, though that was mostly because they had come in smelling distinctly of food. Molly must have smelled like good people, because the beast had already flopped over onto his back to encourage belly rubs. He was a good cat and Molly was a good person. She shouldn't have been surprised that they were already as thick as thieves. Unfortunately, she had to take away his new favorite person.

"Lukers, come here please."

He swished his tail as he wandered to her, gifting her by

rubbing his face across her hands and purring as loud as his body would let him.

"Mommy's going to go away for a few days, but I'm going to come back. I promise. Claudia is going to come and stay with you until I can come home, okay?" She reached to rub his ears, but he wasn't having any of that. He backed away from her without even looking away or pausing his purrs. "I love you, ya jerk. You be good, okay? Claudia will tell me if you aren't."

As if he knew she didn't have anything more to say, he rubbed against her one more time before scampering back towards the bedroom.

"That is such a good cat! You'd never guess how friendly he is from his grumpy little face."

"Absolutely. He's got the grumpiest face and the sweetest soul. Well," she amended. "He's very sweet unless you're a rodent or a laser toy. Those he murders without a worry in the world."

"But of course," Molly said with a laugh. "I would expect no less from such a handsome man. He must provide a wealth of rodents and laser dots for his family or else you will starve."

An image of a plate full of laser pointers came to her and Sofiya laughed. "All right, we can leave now. He's all set and will probably sleep until Claudia comes in tonight."

Molly grabbed Sofiya's purse and handed it to her before taking the handle of the rolling suitcase and making her way out the door.

∾

MOLLY

The first hour of the drive to Richmond was one of Molly's favorite drives. It was all winding, tree-lined roads that barely had any traffic on them. With Sofiya by her side and a rocking playlist playing through the speakers, everything was peaceful. Neither of them said much as they trundled along.

They still hadn't talked about the kiss, but it was almost like they agreed that it had never happened. Except they hadn't, because that would mean that she would have found the courage to talk to the woman about it. Every time she thought she could manage it, something got in the way the same way the knocking on the door had when it happened. She almost thought it was a sign that it wasn't meant to be, but if that were the case, she hoped the universe would cut her a break and let her quit remembering every moment of the too-brief romantic interlude. So far, it had not.

No matter whether she was awake or dreaming, she kept catching herself remembering the way that Sofiya's thick hair had felt against her fingers or the taste of her mouth. Even while she drove, the scent of pomegranate wafted through the car whenever the air conditioning crossed over the older woman. It was simultaneously mouthwatering and intoxicating in a way that she'd never found it to be before.

She clenched her fingers on the steering wheel in an attempt to distract herself from the memory and the lust that came with it, pretending that it was because of the traffic. Unfortunately, there was only so long she could keep that up before her hands tired. She reached for the drink they'd picked up on the way out of town, thinking that maybe caffeine would help her brain to actually function the way it was intended to, but it was stuck in the cup holder. She tried wiggling it, but only succeeded in removing the lid. Luckily, the soda didn't slosh out of the cup when Molly had to brake to avoid hitting someone merging suddenly.

Instead, Sofiya stopped her with a press of her hand and a soft voice. "Here, let me help. You focus on the road."

Seconds later, the soda cup was in her hand. One hand on the wheel, she gratefully sipped it, relishing the cold tang of the Dr. Pepper against her tongue. She went to take another sip when a blue SUV careened into the lane in front of them. Slamming on the brakes and grabbing for the steering wheel with her other hand, she felt the liquid tipping down her arm and

"Fuck!" The curse burst from her lips before she could stop it. She watched the SUV continue on its merry way as if it hadn't almost collided with her. Glancing in the rear-view mirror, she quickly eased the car onto the road's shoulder and forced herself to breathe.

"Molly? Are you okay?"

She held up one cola-soaked finger while she tried to calm her racing heartbeat. It was difficult to do when she could feel her drink sinking into her underwear through her jeans and dripping down her thighs to reach her cloth car seats. It was the most disgusting feeling of wetness she could have imagined. She could feel Sofiya moving around in the car, but she couldn't look at her. She didn't even want to look at herself in that moment.

When she finally felt like her body was under control, she looked at the older woman in her passenger seat. Sofiya was holding out the roll of paper towels that usually lived in her back seat. Molly took them and nearly burst into tears. A few traitorous drops leaked out of the corner of her eyes and Sofiya's face melted into an expression of clear sympathy.

"Oh, honey, it's all right," she soothed. "It's just a little spilled soda."

She couldn't believe how pathetic she must look right now.

"Bet you wish you'd never kissed a girl who can't even stop herself from crying over spilled soda." The words had popped out before Molly could stop them. She wished she could stuff them right back into her mouth, but unfortunately, that wasn't possible.

"Oh, Molly."

She couldn't bring herself to look up, knowing that Sofiya would be looking at her with those soft blue eyes. It would just make her cry even harder and look even more childish. She simply wadded up some paper towels and pressed them into her crotch to soak up the already sticky liquid. It was soaked through almost instantly, but Molly found another wad pressed into her hand before she could pull more off.

"Molly, I know you're upset right now, and I absolutely do

not blame you. I need you to know that I don't regret anything about that night, except that we got interrupted."

Finally, Molly looked up. Sofia's blue eyes were clear and focused on her. She was telling the truth, which surprised her. She wasn't sure why, though. After all, she was the one who had run out of there like something had caught on fire. Something she had regretted herself.

"Really? I thought... I thought it was just a spur of the moment thing." Molly's voice was quiet and despite the emotions roiling in the pit of her stomach, she had stopped crying.

"Just because something happens in the spur of the moment doesn't mean it wasn't a good decision. I had been dreaming of kissing you for months." Her voice was soft but frank. Molly could tell that she was being honest with her and she loved it so much. However, she didn't know how to put her own feelings into words. How did you tell someone that their kiss had meant so much, maybe even everything, when your entire front and backside was covered in Dr. Pepper?

When she didn't answer for a few seconds, Sofiya continued with a more subdued tone. "Now, if you regret it and want to pretend it never happened for yourself, that's your prerogative. But I've been in the world a lot longer than you and I've made it a policy to only kiss people I wouldn't regret it in the morning. I definitely don't risk my job over it."

At that, Molly had to laugh. "You're only ten years older than me. And you've never kissed anyone and regretted it? I find that hard to believe."

A small smile spread across Sofiya's face, making it a little bit easier for Molly to deal with her physical situation. Those laugh lines never failed to make her day a little bit brighter. When she spoke, her voice was much more cheerful. "Oh, I've definitely kissed a few folks I shouldn't have. The policy isn't that old. My point still stands, though. I won't make any more moves towards you since it's clear that you don't want it."

Molly shifted uncomfortably in her squelching seat. That wasn't what she wanted at all. She had to say something and it had to be just right.

"I didn't say I didn't want the kiss," she said quietly. "It was a wonderful surprise. It just... it just surprised me. And overwhelmed me a little. And then I didn't know how to talk to you. So now... here we are, sitting on the side of the road covered in soda."

It was Sofiya's turn to laugh now. She threw her head back and let loose a throaty cackle that made Molly's heart skip a beat.

"Well, we've talked about it now. Sort of. When you're ready to drive, we passed a sign for a truck stop that's a few miles up."

"What, do you need to pee or something? You could have told me."

Sofiya laughed again. "No, though I wouldn't mind stretching my legs. You should be able to give yourself a baby wipe shower there and change your clothes, which I think will make the drive a lot more comfortable."

She was right about that. Molly hated the way her body

felt right then, especially knowing that there was nothing she could do about it right now. A few more miles was much better than another full hour of driving like this, though. She could make it a few more miles. Especially now that the air was clear.

SOFIYA

After what seemed like an eternity in the car, they had finally made it to the hotel that was hosting the conference. Molly was as clean as she could be without a real shower and was in clean clothes, but they were well behind schedule. Because the conference check-in ended before the hotel check in, they brought their suitcases with them to the folding table that was the conference's staging area.

Sofiya tried to stretch her back inconspicuously while Molly gave their names to the bored man sitting behind the table. It didn't work - the crack of her spine almost echoed through the room. She grimaced, but it felt good.

"Andersen and Anderson from the Pittsylvania County Public Library? Here you go." He handed Molly two tote bags that looked full to the brim and two name tags. She handed one of each to Sofiya after glancing at them briefly.

Setting the bag against her suitcase, Sofiya moved to clip the badge to her chest pocket, but paused when she looked at the black text underneath plastic.

"Why does my name tag say 'Mrs.'?" she muttered crankily. She knew she hadn't checked that box.

"What?" Molly looked at her own tag and frowned. "Mine does too. And my last name is misspelled."

"Are you kidding? Your name is super easy to spell." Sofiya turned the other badge so she could see it, and sure enough, it read Mrs. Molly Anderson. She had to push down the rush of warmth that came with seeing Molly's first name with her own last one, reminding herself that this was a professional conference. She couldn't afford to let her feelings get in the way this week. That was difficult, though especially with the smell of Molly's cocoa butter and bergamot lotion filling her nose.

"Oh good lord. People are gonna think we're married. That's... yikes."

It was absolutely useless to go around at a networking event with the wrong name on - no one would know who to look for afterward. Plus, there was the LGBTQ Librarian mixer halfway through the week. Sofiya was hoping to find someone interested in a casual hookup or anything to get her mind off of how much she cared for her coworker. She couldn't very well do that if her name tag made it seem like she was married *to* said coworker.

"Sir?" She raised her voice on the last word, forcing the man to pay attention to them. "Neither of these name tags are correct. Is it possible to get new ones printed or a blank tag to make them for ourselves?"

His bored expression morphed slightly into one closer to indifference, and he shuffled off without saying a word. She guessed he had to have a name as common as dirt, otherwise he would understand the problem here. He returned a moment later with a half-assed apologetic expression. "I'm so sorry, ma'am, but we are unable to do reprinted name tags at this time. All of the tags were printed according to the paperwork that was filled out and we do not have any extras. You will have to make do with the ones or create your own name tag using your own supplies."

His flat tone showed just how little he cared about the matter at hand. Molly's mouth dropped open, while Sofiya raised her eyebrows in incredulity.

"Excuse me? You have *no* extra name tags?" Molly asked, keeping her tone calm but firm. "This is not how my name is spelled, nor is it the correct honorific."

What kind of event planner didn't bring extra name tags? Even if there really were no extras, there was no reason for the man to be such an ass about it. Sofiya's hackles were up now, and they only got worse when the man bristled at Molly.

"There's no need to take a tone with me, ma'am. I'm just doing my job."

"You're the only one taking a tone," Sofiya snapped, stepping forward and looking at his name tag. "Bernard, do you really not have *anything* we can work with to make a professional name tag?"

"Like I said, we do not have any extras because all of them were printed according to the paperwork *you* filled out. You might find pens and notepaper in your tote bags." He had his chest thrown out like he was some sort of hotshot, and his tone was frosty. Sofiya had never given less of a shit about a man's feelings than she did in that moment.

"That was very poorly planned. Thank you for your lack of assistance. Let's go, Molly. We've got to finish checking in so we can make our own name tags." Her voice dripped with condescension and she did not care.

Turning away from him, she caught Molly sticking her tongue out at the man. With a smile, she grabbed her own suitcase and headed for the check in desk. Soon, everything would be fine.

MOLLY

Finally, despite the snafu with the name tags, it was time to check into the rooms. Molly would have killed to just spend a few minutes horizontal and alone before she had to start getting ready for the formal keynote and dinner. All she had to do was get through the check in process and then she'd be blessedly alone.

This time, she was taking over the process. Maybe that would make it go better than the name tag table had. Maybe.

"Hi, I'm Molly Andersen and I'd like to check in for the conference?"

The clerk nodded and began the motions of a check in while Molly pulled the library's credit card out of her wallet.

"Ah, yes, we have your reservation right here, Mrs. Andersen. You and your wife will be in room 401."

Any hope of an easy check in fled with the honorific, and she had to resist the urge to grind her teeth at the use of wife.

"I'm sorry, I believe there has been a misunderstanding. My *coworker* and I are not married and we were supposed to have adjoining rooms, not the same one. Right, Sofiya?" Molly looked back at her coworker and found her with a similarly annoyed expression on her face.

"That is certainly what I put on the paperwork I submitted," Sofiya asserted. "Do you not also have a reservation for Sofiya Anderson? With an 'o' instead of an 'e'?"

The clerk at the desk grimaced and dove back behind their computer, typing and then clicking loudly.

"I'm afraid not, ma'am. The reservation I have on file is for both of you, as it was reserved by the conference team."

Molly groaned. The conference team again. She would have put money on it being the same person who had misspelled her name and marked the Mrs. Box. If she ever found out who that person was, she was going to throttle them. Nothing about this conference was going to plan, and she had no clue how to fix it.

"Do you have another room one of us can check into?" Her voice was desperate. She had struggled with hiding her feelings from Sofiya and at work when she'd had plenty of space of her own to retreat to and a job to do. How was she supposed to keep the feelings from being obvious when they were sharing the same space for four full days?

"I'm afraid all of our other rooms are full," they said patiently. "You must know this conference is a very popular one."

"Does the room at least have two beds?" Sofiya asked, her voice clipped with impatience. "We're two grown professional women. We deserve our own beds, even if our name tags are wrong and we have to share a room."

Molly froze in horror. She hadn't even considered the idea that she might have to share a *bed* with Sofiya. God, she was pretty sure she actually might die. A look of horror fell onto the clerk's well-made up face before they schooled it into a more professional one. Molly knew the answer even before they opened their mouth.

"The room reserved for you has a king bed, but it also features a jacuzzi bathtub and a dual vanity."

Just kill me now, she thought despairingly. The bathtub might be nice but it wouldn't save her from the inevitable death by embarrassment or horniness because for the next four days, she would either be sleeping on the floor or she would be sharing a bed with the woman she hadn't been able to get out of her head for the last 8 months. This was going to go swimmingly.

MOLLY

The hotel's ballroom had been decked out for the keynote dinner and all of its attendees had dolled themselves up accordingly.

The keynote was a rousing speech about the importance of free speech in libraries, which would have been all well and good if the speaker himself had not been one of the people who'd been quoted in all sorts of media about the importance of protecting free speech when hosting transphobes and racists. Molly mostly tuned him out and focused on sneakily watching Sofiya's reactions while they all waited for dinner to be served.

Even after watching her for the whole speech, Molly couldn't get over how beautiful Sofiya was in her dress. The blue silk wrapped her tightly from shoulder to thighs, but sheer shimmering gold fabric covered it, running all the way to the floor into a ball gown. It was simple, elegant, and absolutely stunning on her. If Sofiya never wore another dress in her life, it would be okay with Molly, because she'd have the memory of this one. It was something she was pretty sure she'd never forget, unlike her own tight lavender dress.

"So, how long have you two been married?" One of the other women at their table asked as soon as the speaker was finished, but didn't wait for either of them to answer her. She just flashed her glitzy rings and continued. "You have the look of newlyweds. I remember when my husband and I were newly wed. It was such a wonderful time! We got to go on so many adventures."

Sofiya shot Molly a wry smile before she answered dryly.

"Oh, yes, our 'marriage' is very new. It's certainly an adventure, isn't it, honey?"

Molly laughed in sync with the other woman and bumped her shoulder against Sofiya's bare one in admonishment. She hoped the woman they had just lied to wasn't anyone important. That would be awkward as hell.

"Are you two honeymooning anywhere fun? My husband and I went to Bora Bora this summer for ours." She kept rattling on about how much fun her honeymoon was, not caring that absolutely no one else at the table was listening. Molly barely held in an eye roll. The woman had clearly just wanted to talk about her own recent marriage, which would have been fine under normal circumstances, but she was way too hungry for that right now.

"Sof, will you walk with me to the bar?" She asked softly. Sofiya nodded and excused them both from the conversation. When they were a few feet away, she offered her arm to the woman beside her, who took it. Just that small touch sent tingles all over Molly's body, and she loved it.

"What's up?

"I needed a drink before I had an argument with Karen over there for being a bulldozer. You shouldn't lie to people about our being married, even if they are assholes, you know."

They reached the bar and both women ordered themselves a glass of white wine, then continued their circuit of the room.

That was true. It was funny, but that didn't change the fact that it was a lie. Molly did her best to avoid lying no matter who she was talking to. Even with the kids at work. She had learned a long time ago that lying got her into more trouble than it was worth. She put all of that into words for Sofiya, who sighed and shoved her bangs out of her eyes.

"Fine, we won't lie to people about being married if they ask. But I don't want to go sit back down with Mrs. Talks-A-Lot. Do you want to walk around a little bit before dinner?"

Molly shrugged. "Lead the way."

They wandered around the room greeting people they knew from conferences past or from school. Molly was honestly surprised how many people there were that she recognized. Maybe the world was a little bit smaller than she'd expected, but at least it was a mostly nice one. Finally, they saw the catering staff lining up around the room and made their way back to their own table to be served.

"You know, you look absolutely stunning tonight," Sofiya said nonchalantly just before they reached their table again. "If you were my wife, I'd be proud to be seen with you."

Molly's breath caught in her throat as she smiled tremulously at the woman who she suspected she cared for in a very different way than she'd thought. She couldn't say anything though. Not until she was absolutely sure what her feelings were.

She had learned a long time ago that telling alloromantic

people you had some sort of feelings for them before you were sure those feelings were romantic led them to get ideas and make assumptions that weren't any good. It had burned her in her last three relationships and ruined their friendship as well as the burgeoning romantic one. She wasn't going to let that happen, not again. Sofiya already knew she was attracted to her in some sense. That would be enough for now. It would have to be. All she could do for right now was sit down at the table and eat her dinner without blurting anything too heartfelt out in front of strangers.

SOFIYA

The dinner had been delicious, even if the speech had been ridiculous coming from a useless old man who cared more about making it to retirement than any of his patrons.

Sofiya stared at the white plush comforter with all of the tired wariness that she typically reserved for children who needed to show her something secret. She may have been reasonably assured that there would not be a frog under the covers, unlike most of the children's secrets, but that didn't mean that there was nothing to be wary of - especially when sharing it with a woman she had a hard time controlling herself around.

"So, how do we want to handle this?" Molly asked, apprehension clear in her voice. At least Sofiya wasn't alone in her concerns. "I can sleep on the floor tonight if sharing a bed is a problem for you."

"Don't be ridiculous. Neither of us is young enough to be sleeping on hotel floors," Sofiya scoffed. "We're also adult enough to deal with sharing, right?"

Molly looked at her, her face the picture of stricken anxiety. "Are we?"

Honestly, Sofiya wasn't so sure of that herself, but she did have faith in her pigheadedness. That was a trait that had never failed to show itself.

"Sharing a bed may be a big step for any relationship, but we're professionals, right? We will act like it and we will get the best sleep that we possibly can. Besides, it's huge. How hard can it be to remain on our own sides while we sleep?"

Even as she said it, the plot lines of so many romance novels popped into her head, and she had to shake her head.

"We'll do our best," Molly agreed. "Whatever that winds up being."

That would have to work, she thought as she grabbed her toiletries to take a shower.

MOLLY

The instant the bathroom door closed and locked, I let out a moan that was five percent exhaustion and ninety five percent pure horniness. Having dinner with Sofiya when she'd been so amazing as a panelist earlier in the day was a lot harder than she had expected.

Luckily, she had expected this problem to some extent and thus, had come prepared - pun entirely intended. What the room lacked in a second bed, it made up for with an armchair that would be perfect for her needs.

Laying a hand towel over the seat, she laid out the tools she would need: her favorite vibrator, her unobtrusive wireless headphones, and a particularly titillating section of an erotic audiobook. It was the perfect combination to helping her relieve some of the frustrations that had built up during the day.

Molly shimmied out of the pencil skirt and pink lace panties that had felt like a cage all day and unbuttoned her silk blouse to reveal the matching bralette. She peeled them both over her head and let her braids fall loose around her, reveling in her nudity, her absolute privacy for the first time in more than a day. It was a wonderful feeling, but it was nothing compared to the ecstasy that she was about to bring herself. She put her headphones in and pressed play on the erotic romance she'd chosen for tonight. The narrator's sultry tones filled her ears and as the characters got to business, so did she.

She had years of experience finding the perfect method to get herself hot and ready. Reaching one hand between her legs, she circled her clit with a finger while the other echoed the motion around her left nipple. She held back a moan as the first wave of pleasure rolled through her, then released her breast to reach for the vibrator. She pressed the single button on it until it reached her favorite speed and pulsation.

Letting the tongue-like silicone go to work on her clit, she imagined what it would be like if it were Sofiya's tongue lapping at her juices, if her hands were fisted in Sofiya's hair instead of three of her fingers delving into her slick depths. That thought, the images it conjured, brought her to a shuddering climax mere moments later, and almost all of her troubles melted away with the slick juices leaking onto the chair beneath her. If only something like that would ever happen with Sofiya.

She almost wished that she could spend hours like this, either ministering to herself in one of the best ways possible or letting someone else do it for her. Unfortunately, she had to get dressed to some extent because she had to get back into that bed with Sofiya and act like that didn't send her spiraling into thoughts that were entirely inappropriate to have about her coworker. And in order to do that, she needed to wash her face and act like she hadn't spent the few minutes of alone time taking care of herself. That was totally doable.

FEBRUARY 13

MOLLY

Molly woke up feeling more well-rested than she had felt in years, which was surprising. What was even more surprising was the comforting weight in her arms. She wasn't sure what the feeling was. It felt like a heated weighted blanket all bundled up into one roll that stretched from her chest to her ankles. But she'd left her weighted blanket at home, so that couldn't be it.

Slowly, she realized what the weight was. Opening her eyes, her hunch was confirmed. Sofiya. Her wiry, butch coworker had worked her way into Molly's arms in her sleep and was quietly snoring.

For once, the image didn't make her start instantly lusting after the older woman. Instead, it inspired a softer, more romantic feeling that surprised her. She had known that she liked Sofiya as a potential sexual partner since the day they'd met and as a person shortly after she'd started at the library, but romantic feelings were very different.

If she were being honest with herself, they were also a little scary. She had never begun developing feelings about someone so early on. In fact, she couldn't remember ever having developed romantic feelings for anyone before she'd slept with them. Despite that, she could not have put any other name to the warmth that spread through her veins when she felt the weight of Sofiya in her arms and when she thought of spending more time with her. She was starting to fall in love with Sofiya, and she didn't know how she was going to wrap her head -or her heart- around it.

As if she knew she was being thought of, Molly felt Sofiya suck in a deep breath and stretch in her arms. Suddenly, she didn't know what to do with her limbs. Should she try to extricate herself? Should she pretend to still be asleep? Should she just make a joke out of it? She couldn't just rip her arms away. It could send Sofiya tumbling to the floor if she wasn't careful. But also, she really needed to pee. She couldn't just lay here indefinitely.

Luckily, Sofiya made it so that she didn't have to. Still seemingly asleep, she rolled out of Molly's embrace and almost off the bed. Molly lunged forward and wrapped her arm more tightly around the other woman's warm waist.

"Wha-? Wha's happening?" Sofiya's voice was thick with sleep. Molly felt, rather than saw, the older woman move her head to look at her waist and where she hung precariously halfway off of the bed. "Oh. Shit."

Stiffly, she rolled herself back into the bed with a groan. When she stopped, she was face to face with Molly.

"Well, good morning, ma'am," Sofiya drawled, her eyes still only half open. Molly didn't want to close her own eyes. She wanted to memorize every sensation she felt in that moment, every inch of Sofiya's face.

Her blonde hair was wild from her sleep movement and there were clear crusties in both corners of her eyes and embedded in the fine wrinkles that surrounded them. The neck of the far too large t-shirt that she slept in had shifted to almost fall off of her shoulder. Molly was fairly sure she'd never found her more beautiful than in that moment.

"Good morning," Molly murmured. "Did you sleep well?"

She still sounded groggy, so she cleared her throat as quietly as she could. The sound still felt too loud in the lush quiet bed, but Molly hoped she would sound slightly less like a human frog. Sofiya smiled up at her from the pillows and made a happy sound that sent thrills straight to Molly's core. Man, she had it bad.

SOFIYA

Waking up in Molly's arms had to have been one of the best feelings, particularly because she had not expected it at all.

It had taken hours for her to actually fall asleep the night before simply because she was so unused to sleeping next to anyone other than Luke. A human body was much different from that of a feline, after all. After tossing and turning for a while, she had managed to find the perfect position to sleep in the comfortable bed. However, she was pretty sure that when she had finally fallen asleep, they had both been firmly ensconced in their own burritos of warm blankets.

Apparently, that hadn't lasted. So much for being a professional. So much for keeping her hands to herself. Sofiya couldn't bring herself to be upset about it in the least. Even if it never happened again, it had been worth it. But, God, she hoped that she would find herself back in Molly's arms at some point.

Her alarm jolted her out of her thoughts and she groaned. She had to get herself pulled together and emotionally prepared for a day full of panels and people. She just had to drag herself out of Molly's arms. Sofiya was entirely sure she could do that. Maybe... maybe just in a few more minutes. She could do all of that with just a few minutes less of her morning. It wasn't as if she had planned on doing anything fancy with her hair or makeup, and she didn't need to shower again. Her normal morning routine had been honed to a matter of minutes after she showered, and she was proud of that.

Taking less time getting herself together meant more time for things she enjoyed - usually, a few minutes of extra sleep, time to make and drink her first cup of coffee before she got to the library, and some playtime for Luke before work. Today, she was going to use that explicitly to get just a little more time in Molly's arms.

MOLLY

When they both had made it out of bed finally, they got down to business getting themselves ready for the day. Instead of talking about the way they had woken up, Molly used the restroom, brushed her teeth and pulled her hair out of its protective bun and silk bonnet. Then she took a few minutes to breathe and really think about how this morning had happened.

By the time she'd finished that, Molly could see that Sofiya had pulled out her outfit for the day - one of the navy pantsuits and white silk shirts that she regularly wore to work. She had also gotten partially undressed, to Molly's surprise. She caught the flash of a bare, well-muscled leg before she froze, snapping her eyes shut.

"Uh, Sofiya?"

The older woman whirled around with a gasp. "Shit!"

Molly could hear the whip of the pants in her hands from the force of Sofiya's movement. She almost wished she could see it, see the shock that she knew would be on her face, but she didn't want to invade her privacy. Her personal space was an entirely different story, however.

"You can open your eyes now," Sofiya called. Her voice was full of laughter that brought a smile to Molly's face. When she did so, Sofiya was wearing pants again and her shirt was halfway buttoned. "If I had known you'd be finished so quickly, I would have just waited. I assumed you'd need to do more."

"Nah." Molly shrugged. "I just need a brush of mascara

and lipstick and I'm ready to go. I didn't mean to barge in on you like that…"

"It's fine. Besides…" Sofiya grinned a little wickedly back at her. "I can't say I minded all that much."

Molly laughed loudly, stepping towards her with mischief on her mind. Sofiya had said that she wouldn't make another move until Molly did. What better opportunity could she get?

"You didn't mind, huh?" Her voice lowered to a husky whisper, a voice that she knew would get exactly what she meant across. She could see Sofiya's eyes darken as she understood Molly's intent. She was going to kiss Sofiya and make it clear that she wanted this, wanted some kind of relationship with her, even if it wasn't precisely romantic.

She took several languid steps forward, then stopped suddenly. Sofiya's gaze turned worried.

"Did you hear that?" Molly whispered.

"Hear what?" Sofiya listened, but her expression never dropped the confusion that was evident there. "All I hear is the radiator."

"No, listen. It sounds like there's someone outside our door?"

As if on cue, three swift knocks sounded on the door. Glancing at her phone, she saw it was only 8 a.m. Who could be knocking that early in the morning? What did they want? And why did their kisses have to keep getting interrupted?

≈

SOFIYA

"Mrs. Anderson? Are you in there?" A man's light tenor sounded through the door. Sofiya recognized that voice. It was the annoying man from check-in. Bernard, she thought his name was. Annoying man.

With a sigh, she finished buttoning her shirt and walked to the door, yanking it open.

"It's Ms. Anderson, Bernard. What can I do for you?" Her voice was crisp with annoyance, but honestly she didn't care. This man had been a pain in her ass since before they'd met and he would likely continue to be until she got home.

She heard Molly groan behind her. At least she wasn't the only one annoyed by the situation. She had been pretty sure that Molly had been about to kiss her when things been interrupted yet again and still there was nothing that she could do about it, because fucking Bernard was standing just inside their door.

"Well, now. Doesn't this just look cozy?" Bernard asked, one eyebrow raised as he looked at the bed. "I'm glad you two were happy with the choice of one room instead of two like you requested."

Sofiya could have throttled him. He looked so pleased with himself that he had to have been the one in charge of the room assignments.

"Was that one of your plans then? Along with the name tag snafu?"

"I am not the one who filled out the paperwork, Mrs. Anderson," he said haughtily. "I simply used what information was there to make a decision about what was best given the space we had and the people attending."

He must have been making an effort to use the wrong honorific, she thought while she ground her teeth. There was no way he was actually that incompetent at his job as a conference organizer to actually keep said job.

"What can I help you with, Bernard?" Sofiya repeated. "We have panels to get to."

"Ah, yes. About that." He looked much less confident suddenly, and Sofiya knew that something had not gone according to plan.

She waited for him to continue, eyebrows raised and lips tight against her teeth.

"There is a digital archiving panel at eleven, but one of our two panelists couldn't make it due to some sort of family emergency. So, ah, I came to ask for your help."

Sofiya blinked. He needed her help? And this was the tone he took with her? Men really were something else.

"You want me to take over a panel that I wasn't asked to join? In three hours?" Her voice raised an octave by the end of the second question.

"Well, can you do it?" There was a note of hope in his light voice. Sofiya was tempted to say no, just to be as much of a problem for him as he had been for them over the last few days.

However, she knew digital archiving practices like she

knew her own name. She also knew that many of the rural libraries like theirs struggled to create a system that worked with internet access that was squirrelly at best. That was something that very few other people would be able to bring to the table on such short notice.

Chewing on her lip, she turned to Molly to see what she thought. She found the woman digging in her suitcase, trying to pretend she hadn't been listening to the whole conversation.

"Molly? You think I can pull a panel presentation together in three hours?"

She thought about it for less than a second before loosing a smile so full of confidence Sofiya was almost blown away.

"I'm pretty sure you can do anything you set your mind to. And, if you need help, I'm at your service."

Sofiya grinned back an unspoken thank you before turning back to Bernard, who looked confused more than anything else.

"All right. I'll do the panel, but I will need a few things."

MOLLY

In less than a minute, Sofiya had rattled off everything that she needed and sent Bernard scampering to get it for her. The room felt simultaneously significantly warmer and less crowded without him in it, and Molly was glad to be rid of him.

Molly had asked what Sofiya needed from her, whether it was space to get herself together or assistance, and Sofiya had chosen the latter. Molly wanted to ask what she *wanted* from her, in every sense of the word, but she couldn't ask that. Not now.

Right now, Molly needed to help her put the information into a sensible kind of order for the audience and figure out her, not ask questions that even she wouldn't have wanted to answer in that moment. And that was okay.

While they waited for Bernard to return, Molly pulled a black pencil skirt and mustard colored chevron blouse from the closet, then grabbed the bra she had been looking for in her suitcase and made her way into the bathroom. They had a lot of work to get done in a short amount of time and all of it would turn out better if she were dressed properly for the preparations. Plus, she really didn't want the world's most annoying conference chairman to see her in her nightgown any more than necessary.

"Have you ever done a panel before?" She asked from the bathroom, honestly curious while she slipped out of her blue cotton nightgown and changed into a fresh pair of underwear and bra.

"A few times! Never on such short notice, though. And never for someone so..." Sofiya trailed off. Molly could tell that she was distracted by something, and guessed it was her now-open laptop by the clacking of keys that followed. Molly had an idea of what she would say.

By the time Bernard got back to the room, she was fully dressed and had seated herself on the edge of the bed ready to help. She adjusted her pencil skirt so it was straight - unlike anything else about her - and looked at him. He looked less stressed than he had earlier, but not by much.

"The other panel member's information, the moderators' planned questions, and the general panel description are all on this flash drive, as requested. I also put the emails regarding the panel development into a Word document for you." He held out a pair of business cards and the aforementioned flash drive. Sofiya's hands closed over them and he stepped back. "I will leave you two to it then. Don't hesitate to call if you need anything from me."

When neither woman responded to him, he nodded and walked out of the room without another word. Good riddance, Molly thought.

Sofiya stuck out her tongue at the closed door, and Molly laughed. She loved that they were almost always on the same page with these things.

"All righty then," Sofiya announced as she plugged the drive into her laptop. For some reason, her voice was more Southern than Molly thought she had ever heard it. "Let's do us some learning, shall we?"

The files popped up one by one, overlapping each other and filling the screen. Sofiya double clicked on one and hummed deep in her chest.

"What is it?" Molly asked, her interest piqued.

"Bernard is a smarmy bastard," she mused. "He didn't just bring me what I asked for. He also scanned in our conference applications."

Molly felt her forehead wrinkle as she frowned. "Both of them? Why?"

"I suspect he thinks this will prove his point and explain why he won't quit calling us both 'Mrs.'"

Molly rolled her eyes. As if. Even if Sofiya had misspelled her name and marked them both as married, there was no excuse for Bernard to keep calling them the wrong thing after they had corrected him.

"Oh shit, it might not have been entirely his fault."

"What?" Molly got up and leaned over Sofiya's shoulder to look at the scanned form. Sure enough, there was some sort of discoloration across the top of the form where the honorific checkboxes were. On both forms, the stain looked like a whole lot like the rim of a coffee cup, fully coloring in the "Mrs." box.

"Well, that's embarrassing." Sofiya laughed. "At least your name is actually spelled right on these. That, at least, isn't my fault."

It really wasn't that big a deal, and she told her so, squeezing her shoulder gently. Sofiya leaned her head onto Molly's hand for a moment and let her eyes flutter shut. Molly stopped breathing, afraid that if she did she would lose this contact that warmed her all the way through. She wished she could brush the hair away and press her lips to Sofiya's forehead, but she stopped herself. That would be shockingly intimate and she wasn't sure she was ready for that level of intimacy. She couldn't stop herself from taking a deep breath, enjoying the soft pomegranate smell mixing with her own. It wasn't a scent she had been particularly fond of, but now...

Sofiya interrupted her musings by lifting her head and sighing softly. The loss of contact was almost painful, even though Molly knew that was a ridiculous thing to be upset about.

"Ready to get started?" Sofiya asked.

"I'm ready for anything," Molly replied. She was surprised to realize that when it came to Sofiya, that was actually true. Even more surprising was the fact that it didn't really bother her. But, as always, there wasn't time to focus on that. There was work to be done.

SOFIYA

By the time the panel had ended, Sofiya was surprised that she hadn't fallen asleep at the table. She loved talking about the intricacies of digital archiving, especially when it came to library work, but she was *exhausted*.

That was the first time she'd ever been assigned, planned and conducted a panel all in one day and she hoped that she never, *ever* had to do it again. It wasn't the way she liked to work. She much preferred to slowly gather her thoughts and actually put together a memorable presentation.

Luckily, the attendees seemed to enjoy it. There had been lots of questions - most of them good - so maybe she'd shared a little bit of her knowledge with the greater librarian population of the East Coast. She thought she'd seen Molly slip in for the later half of it, which had buoyed her spirits more than she'd expected, but she didn't see her rainbow braids anywhere in the crowd now that the panel was over.

Instead, person after person came up to ask her a question or get her contact information so they could ask her questions later. It was flattering, really, especially because they weren't asking anything of her fellow panelist. She would feel bad, but honestly, she wasn't sure how he had gotten on the panel in the first place except to maybe make whoever she replaced look even more knowledgeable by comparison.

Eventually the line to talk to her cleared and the conference staff began rearranging the chairs and tables for the next panel that needed it. She went to get her bag from where she left it and found a small note folded on top of it.

"Had to run to another panel while you were busy being admired. You were amazing! See you at dinner!" The note was signed with a flourished M. She didn't know when how Molly had gotten back here without her noticing, but she was glad she had. It was such a sweet little gesture that made her heart swell with joy.

Looking at her own schedule, she realized that she didn't have any other panels she wanted to attend on today's schedule. She was glad for that, because she desperately needed something to eat. She had missed breakfast thanks to the change of plans, and she had regretted it all morning.

She picked up her bag and headed towards the lobby with a light heart and an empty stomach. There were all sorts of restaurants within walking distance, and with a little help from the staff, she was sure to find something delicious. And then, perhaps, she'd take advantage of having the room to herself and have herself a good old-fashioned nap.

MOLLY

Molly's afternoon was just as much of a whirlwind as the morning had been, except with a little less Sofiya in it. Her body kept forgetting that she wasn't by her side.

When she heard something interesting, she turned to her left, where Sofiya would have been if she'd been there. Whenever a panel drifted into questions that didn't pertain to her, she found herself wondering what Sofiya was doing. Then she rolled her eyes and focused back on the panel. After all, the people who had made the conference possible had paid good money for her to come out here and learn, not to sit and moon over someone who she hadn't managed to properly make a move on at all.

Of course, the world kept getting in the way of these things. The closest she had gotten to doing so was in her sleep, which was just embarrassing. She couldn't remember ever being this flustered around any of the other women and she had dated over the years, even the ones she had been in love with. Of course, she hadn't wanted anything other than sex from most of those women. That, at least, she knew she was good at. She just had to, you know, get there.

Shaking her head at herself, she tried to focus on the

discussion happening on stage in front of her. Four middle grade authors were talking about their books and how to deal with hard subjects with such a vulnerable population - and their parents. It was something she had struggled with while trying to make story time and kid's book club choices.

It was funny that she was sitting here listening to Kelly Yang talk about some of the push-back she had gotten from parents and librarians alike about her book *Front Desk*. As a very rural county, Molly had thought it would be a great choice for the middle school book club and gotten it approved by her boss. Dealing with immigration was something that many of these farmer's kids were already dealing with, but the response from parents had been surprisingly horrible.

She'd been complained about and called more names than even the middle schoolers could have come up with for each other. For once in her life, those names hadn't had anything to do with her race or her sexuality because most of the people literally hadn't seen her yet. One of the ones calling her names was even one of the members of the Board of Supervisors, which had stung.

Judging by what Yang was saying, she wasn't the only one that had experienced this. Parents didn't want their kids knowing about the realities of the world when those realities weren't sunshine and rainbows. Even when their kids already saw those realities every day. Maybe even especially then, Molly thought.

She could somewhat understand the sentiment. After all, what parent wants their ten-year-old to know that the world is fundamentally broken and not everyone has the stability they have? But when the people working on their family's farm were so similar to the people on the pages they hid from their kids, it became something different, something much more harmful. Kids nowadays were smarter, and more informed than their parents realized. When their parents wanted them to hide their heads in the sand like ostriches, that was when other adults needed to step in.

It was up to the teachers and librarians in their lives to make sure they got all the information they could, which Molly had been glad to find that the library leadership believed as well. Instead of using it as their book club book, it had been their display book and been featured in all of their newsletters for the month. It was still one of their most checked out books months later, particularly by the kids she'd intended to read it with, to her absolute delight. It had become her small, petty revenge to make sure that the most liberal and diverse of books made it into kids' hands. That was something Sofiya had been helping her with, and one of the things that had brought them together. She wished she could have been here for this panel, of all of the ones she was attending throughout the day. It just would have made things better.

Then a calendar notification popped up on her phone, reminding her that their dinner plans were in an hour, and it was like someone lit a candle in her mind. Everything seemed just that much better when she realized she would still get to share it all with the woman she cared for.

~

SOFIYA

Sofiya was the first to arrive at Bookbinders, since she had had no other commitments for the afternoon, so she let herself be seated and then texted Molly to tell her where to find her.

Molly sent back a message saying she was on the way and then Sofiya put her phone away. Instead of scrolling through social media messages she didn't care about, she looked around the former tobacco warehouse. The scent of dried tobacco still hung around the brick walls but it only added to the beautiful scent of the steak, seafood and delectable side dishes people were eating all around her. Black and white photos of fish and old-timey Richmond were carefully matted and framed on the walls, lit by racks of lighting. The overall effect was stunning, even before she saw the food being served.

A waiter walked past with a bowl of lobster macaroni and cheese in one hand and a crab-stuffed salmon fillet that made her tongue tingle with mere anticipation. Another waiter walked past with even more food and she had to stop herself from drooling over it. By the time Molly arrived, she had been delivered a bergamot and earl grey infused cocktail that was keeping her from ordering every single thing on the menu that sat in front of her.

"This place is beautiful," Molly said as she slid into the booth. She wasn't wrong, but suddenly, Sofiya wasn't looking at anything around them. The simple pencil skirt and blouse that had been entirely appropriate for the day somehow hit her a lot differently in the restaurant's simple lighting.

"You look really lovely today. I don't think I mentioned that earlier."

"Oh, thank you!" Molly tilted her head towards her chin in a motion that Sofiya recognized as bashful. "I really love the way this color makes my skin look."

It warmed her skin beautifully, Sofiya noticed. She was about to say so when the waiter arrived.

"Is your party complete, ma'am?" Sofiya nodded and he continued. "I'm glad to hear it. Now, let me tell you about what we have for you today."

He rattled off the specials, then reminded them that Bookbinders had seafood "straight from the fisherman to the kitchens" and would be extra tasty because of it. Then he left them to their own devices to decide what they wanted to order.

Sofiya found it much more difficult to focus on the menu in front of her when she felt Molly's legs pressing up against hers beneath the table. Luckily, everything on the menu looked good and almost everything was well within their allowed budget, thanks to not needing to pay for breakfast or lunch at the hotel. Instead of looking at the menu, she surreptitiously watched Molly read over her own, flitting her eyes back to her own space whenever the other woman looked up at her. She thought of ordering the oysters, then remembered that they were an aphrodisiac. She couldn't help but think she didn't need any help in that department tonight.

Eventually, they chose an order of the lobster macaroni and cheese and silver dollar mushrooms to share, the crab cake stuffed salmon and the sesame crusted yellowfin tuna for their dinners. Molly also asked for a glass of sangria, which came out with the appetizers. Sofiya got another drink for herself simply because the first one was so good. It also gave her something to focus on other than the woman sitting across from, who was watching her with a question written on her face. Clearly, she had missed something.

"I'm sorry, did you say something? I was lost in thought." Lost in lust was more like it, she thought as she blushed, but she didn't need to tell Molly that.

Molly laughed and leaned forward. Sofiya couldn't help but notice how the notch in her blouse's collar revealed just a little bit more of her cleavage with the movement. "I asked how you thought your panel went. I was impressed by what I saw."

"Oh, it went well. I wish I could have gone a little more in depth, but I got a lot of great questions, so I guess I piqued their interest a little. Maybe they'll go home and be a little more careful with their digital metadata practices. Maybe they won't, but I did the best I could."

While she spoke, the waiter arrived with their appetizers and drinks. It all looked and smelled delicious, and she couldn't wait to dig in, but Molly stopped her by raising her glass.

"To helping people learn," she toasted. Sofiya raised her own glass and drained the half-empty glass. It really was refreshing despite -or maybe because of- the high level of alcohol that she could taste in it.

"Did you have fun in your other panels?" Sofiya asked as

she dug into the mac and cheese. "Oh my god, you've gotta try this."

Molly did so, daintily picking through the small dish to make sure she had the perfect ratio of lobster to macaroni, plus a little extra sauce. It was adorable.

"I wouldn't say it was fun, but it was definitely educational," Molly said around bites of food. "I kept thinking you would have enjoyed it, but you weren't there to see it."

"Ah, sorry, I was up in our room taking advantage of having the bed to myself."

"What, you don't like sleeping with me?" Molly said indignantly. Sofiya whipped her head up only to find a wide grin on her face. So she'd decided to be a tease tonight, huh? Well, two could play at that game.

"There are some things a girl just shouldn't do with another person in the bed, unless that person wants to join in. It's just impolite."

She blinked at what she said. Had she really just cracked a masturbation joke? Apparently the booze was also lowering her inhibitions. Not that that was necessarily a bad thing. Molly's grin remained steady and she breathed a sigh of relief.

As if the universe knew they were just getting started, their entrees arrived smelling like heaven. The salmon was perfectly pink and flaky, while the yellowfin tuna looked like something out of a magazine. Apparently Molly thought the same thing, because she pulled her phone out and snapped a photo of it.

After that, they both dug in, falling into a companionable silence punctuated by happy moans and the sound of chewing.

"You've got to try this. It is fantastic," Molly moaned. "I see why everyone raves about them."

She sliced a piece of the sesame crusted, dark magenta tuna steak and swiped it through the spicy coleslaw that and slid it onto her fork, then held it out to Sofiya. As daintily as she could, she allowed herself to be fed.

Molly was right. It was absolutely divine. Sofiya had never had rare tuna before, but this was definitely something she would have to have again. The crunch of the sesame against the heat of the coleslaw made the perfect bed for the very mildly flavored fish. She also understood why it was called a steak instead of a fillet. It was firm in her mouth, the same way that a beef steak would have been, and it was *delicious*.

"Okay, you definitely win the best order tonight," Sofiya said after she'd finished her bite. "I'm gonna have to see if Claudia can make that, because that is *killer*."

Molly laughed. "I hope it's not *a* killer. Though, if it is, at least I got to spend my last night on Earth in good company."

That warmed Sofiya's heart. "Uh, death is absolutely not allowed, ma'am. I would be scarred and heartbroken forever."

Her cheeks warmed as she realized what she had said. She was lucky that Molly already liked her, because she was making a fool of herself. Going back to her own food, she jumped when she felt a foot slide around the back of her leg.

Molly continued eating as if everything was normal, but Sofiya saw her gaze flit upward to meet hers before going back to the table. She really was a tease tonight. If this was her way of making a move and not letting anyone interrupt them, Sofiya was definitely a fan.

She watched Molly continue eating as if she wasn't rubbing her bare foot along the length of Sofiya's calf.

"Everything taste all right for you tonight, ladies?"

Molly glanced at Sofiya as if waiting for her to answer.

"Everything is absolutely perfect," Sofiya answered the waiter, but kept looking at Molly. She lowered her gaze back to the table, but her smile made it clear that she understood that Sofiya was talking to her, too.

"Well, when y'all are finished, I've brought out the dessert menu for your perusal. I personally recommend the chocolate lava cake, but you might also enjoy the apple crostata with vanilla bean ice cream."

Both desserts sounded delicious, but Sofiya was so full that she couldn't even think of eating. That didn't mean that Molly was, though.

"What do we think about dessert?" Sofiya asked thoughtfully. Molly blinked, as if she was surprised by the question.

"Honestly, Sof, I'd rather get out of here and have you for dessert back at the hotel."

Molly's eyes widened, as if she was surprised by her own

statement. Sofiya froze, her foot curled around Molly's leg. She couldn't have heard her right.

"Did you just say you wanted to have me for dessert?" Sofiya asked. Her voice cracked halfway through, like a nervous schoolboy but she didn't have the energy to care. She needed to know what she had actually said.

"Yes. I want to go back to this hotel room and use that bed for what it was made for." Her voice was steady, but Sofiya could see the way her eyes had tightened. She also hadn't lifted her eyes from her drink. She was more nervous than she was letting on. "Is that something you're interested in?"

"God, you have no idea. I'll pay the bill if you'll go get a cab."

Molly nodded, grabbed her purse and walked to the front of the restaurant. Sofiya waved down the waiter. No one had ever been so direct with her before, telling her exactly what she wanted. It was the sexiest thing anyone had ever done for her and there was no way she was going to miss this chance.

MOLLY

The Uber ride back to the hotel was almost painful as they tried their best to keep their hands off of each other.

They nearly ran to the elevator, hands clasped so tightly that Molly thought her fingers might break. It was a good thing because if they hadn't been, Molly would have been using her hands to explore every inch of Sofiya's body the way she had been dreaming of for so long.

Once the elevator doors closed behind them and began to ride, all their inhibitions dropped to the floor below them. Molly looked up at the older woman and found her staring right back at her with a hunger that echoed her own. Sofiya pulled her close and used her own body to push Molly back against the cool metal of the doors until there was no space between them. Sofiya began to trail hot, wet kisses down her neck and Molly lost all sense of everything that existed outside of their bodies.

The minute that it took to get them from the lobby to their fourth floor room was simultaneously too short and too long. Too short for them to truly explore each other the way they so desperately wanted to, but too long for them to hold themselves back from touching each other as much as physically possible.

She was only dimly aware of the ding that signaled they'd reached their floor, but Sofiya held her so tightly that there was no chance of falling. Forcing herself to use her legs for more than the jelly they wanted to be, she led them back to the bedroom door. She swiped the card and tried to open the door, only to find that the handle blinked red at her. Grunting, she swiped again and it opened just as Sofiya's lips found hers again.

They nearly tumbled over each other in their rush to get to the bed that had been the source of such conflict only three days before. Molly would have marveled at the fact that it had been only three days if she hadn't been preoccupied with figuring out how best to get Sofiya out of the suit that had been driving her crazy all day.

She flung the blazer away and focused her trembling fingers on the tiny buttons of her [color] blouse. She wanted to see her, all of her, but there were so many god-damned buttons in the way.

Laughing softly, Sofiya started from the bottom of her own blouse and helped Molly finish removing the garment.

Sofiya's fingers were firm and steady as she slid the zipper of Molly's dress down. Shrugging out of it, Molly stood before Sofiya in nothing but her kitten heels and, thankfully, a matching black bra and black cotton and lace panties.

Sofiya had gone still at the sight of her but even in the dark, Molly could feel her gaze as it traveled from her face down to her toes and all the way back up. She'd thought she would feel vulnerable, but instead, she felt powerful.

"God, you're beautiful," Sofiya murmured, a look of wonder on her lined face.

Molly could have said the same for Sofiya. She was certainly thinking it. She was still half clothed, but Molly loved every inch of what she could see. Her pale pink bralette couldn't hide the way her nipples stood erect, just begging someone to suck on them. The way she stood there in her grey suit pants with just a little bit of her stomach poking out as her chest heaved with exertion and attraction was one of the most beautiful sights Molly thought she had ever seen. She just *had* to see the rest of her.

Molly let herself drop gently to her knees on the rough carpet and dipped the fingers of both hands behind

Sofiya's waistband. The older woman's hips jerked at this simple touch, and Molly looked up.

"May I?"

Sofiya only nodded, but Molly could feel her breath quickening beneath her fingers. Sliding her fingers to the buttons, she undid the pants and pressed a kiss to the place where they had dug into Sofiya's flesh during the day. As she worked them the rest of the way down her legs, she trailed kisses along the lines of her muscles, refusing to let a single moment go to waste. Each kiss made Sofiya moan just a little bit louder.

Sofiya kicked off her shoes and stepped out of the pants, allowing Molly to push her gently backwards until she fell onto the plush comforter with a soft oof.

They had finally made it to the bed and she found herself with Sofiya's pussy right in front of her, only separated by a thin blue strip of fabric and a few inches of air. The scent of her pomegranate soap mixed with the warm scent of her arousal was intoxicating. Sofiya tossed her a pillow and she slid it under her knees, marveling that even at a time like this the woman was still focused on making sure she was okay.

"May I?" she asked again, and Sofiya breathed out a "yes" so softly that Molly felt its vibrations more than she heard the word.

Molly kissed her way deeper between the older woman's well-muscled legs, loving the sharp intake of breath and sigh that came when her nose brushed against her damp panties. Gently, she tugged the underwear away and let them drop to the floor. Just as gently, she moved forward and gripped Sofiya's thighs with one hand. The other traced the lines of her lips, circling her clitoris with the soft pad of her thumb, then plunged her middle finger into her slick depths. She found a rhythm that set Sofiya gasping and rocking with every movement, then added a second finger.

"Yes," she repeated. "*Yes.*"

As they moved together, Molly ached to taste her, to learn the secrets of her most intimate places. When Sofiya bucked forward towards her hand and her face, she allowed her tongue to flatten and soften, to gently reach for every one of those secrets, and she loved what she found. With every light lick, she took in a little bit more of her juices as she went back and forth between them and the clitoris.

"More. Faster." Sofiya moaned. "Please."

Molly was only too happy to oblige. Using her hands to spread Sofiya's legs even further apart, she replaced her fingers with her tongue, licking at the spot that Sofiya clearly enjoyed the most while her nose rubbed against her clitoris at the same pace. It wasn't long before Sofiya's walls and thighs were shaking and shuddering with pleasure around Molly.

"Don't stop." Sofiya pressed her hand to the back of Molly's neck to hold her in place while she came in shuddering gasps. "God, never stop."

Lapping at the juices that came in waves and reveling in the joy of the moment, Molly couldn't imagine being anywhere else. When she came up for air, Sofiya was looking at her like she was the entire world and Molly couldn't remember the last time she had felt so beautiful.

Sofiya wrapped her hands around the back of her arms and pulled her forward gently until their bodies were pressed against each other. The contact was intoxicating in a way that even the drinks at dinner couldn't match. Molly pushed forward to kiss Sofiya, hard and deep and thought she might cry at how good it felt to kiss her with the taste of her orgasm still on her tongue.

Sofiya pulled her to one side so that she straddled one of her muscular legs. Molly's pussy hummed with pleasure at the contact, at the way Sofiya still rocked, putting painful, beautiful pressure on them both. She loved having her hands, her mouth, her everything on Sofiya's body. Her small, firm chest heaved with every motion, pushing her breasts into Molly's.

Before long, Molly found herself fully straddling Sofiya's lap. The older woman had snaked a hand down between them to tease her clit with gentle fingers. With every stroke, she got closer and closer to Molly's wet heat and brought her closer to the edge. A cry ripped out of her before she could stop herself, and Sofiya captured both it and her mouth in a hungry kiss, as if she wanted to eat her face instead of the dinner they'd barely finished.

When she came, Molly lit up from the inside. It was like fireworks were going off inside of her as the walls of her pussy contracted around Sofiya's fingers as they rubbed against her g-spot. God, it felt so good. There were many things a toy could do, but even her trusty vibrator couldn't act as a substitute for a real woman. Especially not one as stunning as Sofiya. By the time the waves had ceased,

Molly was breathing just as heavily as she rolled onto the bed beside the woman who had just fucked her senseless. Sofiya fell back to lay beside her, tangling their fingers together in an echo of the grip that they'd held all the way home from the restaurant.

For the first time in eight months, Molly felt at peace beside Sofiya, so happy she could burst. She didn't know what their future held, but for right now, everything felt perfect.

FEBRUARY 14

SOFIYA

The two women woke up tangled in each other's arms again, but they made it out of bed relatively on time and to the hotel's cafe before the breakfast rush for the first time during their stay. Of course, they only got there because they didn't talk about Every tray of the full breakfast buffet was labeled with what ingredients were local and which businesses had provided them and the space was actually kind of cozy feeling, despite stretching halfway across the hotel lobby.

Molly loaded up on eggs, toast and a glass of orange juice while Sofiya chose to grab herself two cups of coffee, a bagel smeared with cream cheese and a few slices of bacon. Molly raised an eyebrow at the amount of caffeine, but Sofiya wasn't going to let the judgment cloud her enjoyment of her creamed and sugared beverages.

"I'm old. I need more caffeine to function than you do.

Now hush and eat your food." She punctuated her statement with a loud slurp. Molly just shook her head at Sofiya and tucked in. Before long, Sofiya felt much more human and was able to start eating her bagel.

The second full day of the conference was due to be an even busier one than the previous, though she hoped it would be a lot less stressful, especially given the number of orgasms she'd had in the last twelve hours. Conferences were great as mini vacations, but she loved getting to learn new things to bring back home more than she loved the break from the day to day work.

As the only full weekend day of the conference, Sofiya knew it was going to be packed by librarians and publishing industry people alike. She intended to make the best use of it she could by making as many quality contacts as she could. Normally, it would be Sarita's job to wrangle new presenters or non-library and programs, he had asked them to do it in her place this year since she wasn't there.

Molly would be doing the same thing, though she had said she planned to go to some of the more educational panels for children's literature. This conference was great for finding new authors and ensuring that their books were accessible to as many people as possible, especially for kids.

She opened her mouth to ask Molly how she was feeling the night before, but stopped herself when Molly's eyes left her face and flitted to something just above it.

"Well, fancy meeting you two here," a familiar voice said

just before a hand clapped down on Sofiya's shoulder. She choked, trying not to spit the bite of bagel she had just taken across the table at Molly, whose eyes were round with surprise and what she suspected was a little bit of horror. Where did she know that voice from?

Turning her head, she recognized the massive class ring on a hand that had to belong to Chad Dawes. Now she completely understood Molly's face. He was the current Chairman of the Board of Supervisors, and frankly, he was a massive dick. He was the very worst of the local Republicans and the least likely to vote for anything that even vaguely resembled something the community needed. Sofiya could not imagine what could have brought him to this hotel in Richmond at the same time as a librarian conference.

Despite the fact that being in the same room with this many employed women had to be giving him hives, he was grinning toothily at them.

"Mr. Dawes. What a surprise!" Molly said, as diplomatically as she could have. Sofiya knew she hated the man after the stunt he'd pulled with her book club choice. "What are you doing in Richmond?"

"Well, I was in town and heard there was a librarian conference, Ms. Sofiya," he drawled. "Y'all know I'm always trying to get a little more involved in everything our county holds dear, so I thought I'd come and see what fun I could find, and look who I found."

God, he really was a bastard. Watching Molly out of the corner of her eye, she could see her thick lips flatten into a line. Before she could speak, the man continued.

"Oh, but I don't think I've met your friend. Or is this your wife? I see you've changed your name tag to 'Mrs.' Now."

God damn Bernard and these stupid badges, she thought as he squeezed her shoulder again. She hadn't known to fear this particular situation, but this was exactly the kind of thing they had both worried about with the name tags. Looking across the table, she saw that same fear in the wrinkle between Molly's thin eyebrows as they pressed together.

"No, we are not married, Mr. Dawes," she informed him. "There were some issues with making the badges this year and they messed ours up. This is our children's librarian, Molly Andersen. I believe you're familiar with some of the work she's done since she got here."

"Ah, yes. I am familiar with Molly's work," he said dryly. "It's a pleasure to meet you, Molly. I hope you've been enjoying your time in Pittsylvania County and here at this fine conference."

"Oh, I have been," Molly said brightly. "I've learned so much already that I can't wait to hear what the rest of the day has to hold! There are so many new books out there for us to buy to help and make sure every child in our library has a well-rounded view of the world."

Sofiya bit her tongue to stop herself from laughing out loud at the quickly covered look of horror that crossed his darkening face at her words. It was the exact right thing to say to horrify him but also nothing he could actually get upset in public over.

God, she loved everything about Molly. She had always known that she was so beautiful it drove Sofiya to distraction, and so smart that she put almost everyone around her to shame, but the way she quietly but firmly stood up to a man that could very easily make her life a living hell... that was the sexiest thing she had ever seen.

She could only hope that he wouldn't take revenge on Molly later. She didn't think that there was anything that he could use against her. Except... Cold washed over her. Could he somehow tell what had happened last night?

There is no way that he really could have known, she thought, trying to calm herself. The man had a habit of knowing way more than he should when it came to people he didn't like and he had never liked Sofiya. He certainly didn't like Molly, despite never having met her before.

She took a few deep breaths, trying to be stealthy, as Mr. Dawes pulled up a chair and joined their table.

"You know, I had been wanting to talk to you girls. I understand that you have a problem with the planned budget changes and you're forming some kind of campaign against the board."

Now they had gotten to the real reason he was here. He didn't like that anyone dared speak up against him, even though they hadn't really.

"We are not doing anything like that," Molly informed him plainly. "You wouldn't be happy if someone told you your salary and budget were getting slashed for the third year in a row, but we aren't forming a campaign against anything. All we did was put together a video montage of all of the things that our visitors appreciate about the library. Not to mention, it didn't cost the county a penny other than our regular salaries. We did half the work on it outside of work."

"I admire your dedication to the work," Dawes drawled. "That doesn't change the fact that y'all made it specifically to manipulate the board into not cutting your budget. Am I wrong?"

He wasn't, and he knew it. However, it wasn't the only use for the video.

"It will be great for short- and long-term marketing," Sofiya informed him. "Our social media team is already working with it to create advertisements that they can use online. Which, again, is absolutely free outside of what the county is already paying us to do. You run a business, right?"

He squinted at her, trying to figure out her angle. "I do. Why?"

"Then you know how expensive advertising is. We are doing what we think is right, so that hopefully the board will see the value in what we do and the impact we have on the people of this community. I don't see how there is anything wrong with that."

Her last statement was met with a loud silence from Mr. Dawes and a toothy grin from Molly. There was a ringing truth about it. There was absolutely nothing wrong with what they were doing - both on the library's behalf and what they were doing together. She wished she could grab Molly's hand under the table, but knew that he would see the movement. She couldn't give them away like that. Not now.

"I don't have an issue with y'all making marketing materials," Dawes drawled. "My issue is that those materials are going to be used to make my life harder during this budgeting process. I don't like it when people make my life harder."

Molly raised her eyebrows at him. "Forgive me if I've misunderstood the budgeting process here in the county, since I arrived after the last one had finished, Mr. Dawes, but I thought that was what all of the departments were supposed to do. Make our cases for why we shouldn't get our budgets cut and what we need to serve the citizens. That's why Sarita was supposed to show it to you as part of her presentation later today... Hang on, how did you see the video already?"

His smile was so sharp and thin that Sofiya thought she could have embroidered with it.

"I'm the chairman of the board, sweetheart. I see everything that happens in and around our county." She bristled at the use of the pet name and knew that he saw it. Nevertheless, he continued, with a much colder voice than before. "I made a promise to the people that voted for me that I would get them the best bang for their buck. Our county is spending too much money on frivolous things that people should be able to afford on their own, including many of the things your library provides. No matter what you two think you are going to accomplish with this video and this presentation, you are not going to win. If you keep fighting us on this, you are not going to like the results."

Sofiya was stunned into silence as he rose from the table,

buttoned his jacket and strode away. That was the most blatant threat she had ever heard him make.

"What. The Fuck. Was that?" Molly asked, her jaw clamped tightly around the words the instant he was out of earshot.

"That... is going to be a problem." Sofiya murmured, watching him go. "He was absolutely not kidding. We're going to have to watch our backs."

MOLLY

Molly couldn't remember ever feeling so off-kilter in a room full of fellow librarians and publishing people. Sure, this event was larger than any she had attended in grad school, but that wasn't the problem.

The problem was that, yet again, she and Sofiya had taken a huge step in their relationship and they hadn't talked about it. She'd tried to bring it up before they left the room, and she thought Sofiya had been about to say something at breakfast before Chairman Dawes had shown his ugly face.

His presence made her nervous, and his threats made it even worse. He wasn't supposed to be there. He wasn't supposed to have seen the video. He certainly wasn't supposed to have taken it as a threat to his manhood, or his voters or whatever he had decided it was.

Yet again, she found herself worried for her job. Realistically, she knew that they couldn't fire her. The board did not have those powers and Sarita wouldn't go along with some trumped up issue.

However, there was the issue of Sofiya and what they had done last night. Until this moment, she had had absolutely no regrets about the evening's activities, or the next mornings. What if he somehow knew about what they had done? Her boss might not have an issue with it, but the rest of the county...

Sarita's comment about the new dating policy at work floated back to her.

"The county has begun changing its policies to disallow relationships between employees who work in the same department or together," their boss had informed them.

Technically, Sofiya worked in a separate department but they worked the same shifts at the same branch. Would that count against her? She had no idea, and that terrified her.

She needed to talk to Sofiya and figure out what the hell they were going to do.

SOFIYA

Molly found her wandering through the booths on the exhibition hall floor, panic written all over her face. She grabbed Sofiya's arm in a grip so tight it almost hurt.

"Sof, what if he knows? We're technically not supposed to even date, let alone sleep together. Especially not on a work trip where we're both technically on the clock..."

Molly was clearly spinning out. Sofiya tried to interrupt, though whether she wanted to offer some words of wisdom or comfort, she wasn't sure. When her third attempt to interrupt Molly failed, there was only one solution.

Sofiya kissed her, not caring a bit but they were in a crowded room full of librarians and publishers. Molly froze in shock then fell into the kiss as if it were the only thing she could do, wrapping her arms around Sofiya and relaxing - probably for the first time since breakfast.

Someone behind them wolf whistled, and that was enough to bring them both back to their senses.

"Get it, girl!" A man she didn't know called from somewhere in the room, to a chorus of laughter from one part of the room and boos from another. Men were the fucking worst.

"Keep it moving, perv!" Sofiya flipped him off and took Molly's hand in both of hers. "C'mon. Let's go somewhere private."

Molly nodded and led the way back to the elevator, where she leaned against Sofiya as it rose up to their room. The whole way there, she rubbed her thumb in circles over the web between Molly's thumb and forefinger. It seemed to calm her a little by the time she swiped her card in the door. It certainly helped Sofiya feel a little more in control.

Before they'd even walked in, she could tell by the lemony smell of the room that housekeeping had been there. The bed was made again, which meant that there was no further evidence of their activities, the night they had shared together. It felt like a loss, somehow, to see it returned to its state of normalcy. Sofiya shook her head, knowing that was ridiculous, and turned her attention back to Molly.

"Before we talk about the Dawes issue, I have a question." Molly said, chewing on her bottom lip. Sofiya knew she shouldn't find that sexy, but she did.

"Go for it."

"Do you regret last night? I know you were kind of drunk and—" Sofiya cut her off, seeing the fear starting to creep back into her beautiful face. She wouldn't allow that when there was something she could do about it.

"Whoa there. Hey, come here." She pulled Molly into her arms, resting her head on her shoulder. Molly breath left her chest in a whoosh. "You know my policy. I don't regret a single thing about last night - or this morning, for that matter."

"Really?" She lifted her head and looked Sofiya in the eye.

"Really. I've been dreaming about what being in bed with you all would feel like for months."

"And how did it measure up?" Her mouth lifted into a smirk and Sofiya smiled in return.

"Better than I could have ever imagined. And I have a *great* imagination." That got her a full blown smile, one that was as warm as the summer sun. She basked in it, letting it lift her out of her own funky headspace.

"How about you? Do you have any regrets?" Sofiya asked

in return. "It's okay if you do, especially after the threat this morning."

Molly shook her head, still smiling. "You weren't the only one imagining how great it would be. That being said, I also really, *really* don't want to lose my job. Do you know how hard it is to find somewhere that pays a living wage and is close enough to visit my family?"

"Believe it or not, I do. However, they would have to do some real good digging to find anything worth firing us for," Sofiya pointed out. "At worst we've broken a brand new HR policy by a mere technicality. Remember, we don't technically work in the same department of the library system."

"Yes, but that's just a technicality-" Molly tried to say.

Sofiya interrupted her. "And in another, I'm technically your senior, which would put me at fault for all of this."

"As if I'm going to sit here and let you take the blame for this," Molly snorted. "That would get you slapped with a sexual harassment notice in your file that would definitely follow you to whatever your next job was. And it would mean we probably couldn't be together in the long run, if you had to leave."

That dropped into the room like a lead balloon. There was no denying that that was the truth of it. If either of us were to get fired, there was no way we could stay in the county. I might be able to get a job at one of the local colleges or in a surrounding locality, but that would be the best possible outcome.

"So, what do you want to do?" Sofiya asked, honestly at a

loss. There were a few options that she could see: ignore the issue and let the cards fall where they may; end their relationship and call it a one night stand, which wouldn't necessarily protect either of them; or get ahead of the issue and tell Sarita exactly what was going on with Chairman Dawes, and with the two of them.

Sofiya laid the cards out, hoping Molly saw something else that they could do. Molly took a few deep breaths while she thought it through. Then she nodded.

"I think we need to talk to Sarita. As soon as humanly possible."

MOLLY

Sofiya clicked Sarita's name and put her phone on speaker. Setting it on the desk between them, they twined their fingers together and listened to the dial tone.

She hated almost everything that had brought her to this point - worried for her job and worried for her budding relationship in addition to being worried about what the fuck her feelings were toward Sofiya.

She loved spending time with the other woman, and thought she was one of the most attractive people she'd ever seen, but there was a warmth and depth to the feelings that was something she didn't usually feel. If she was being honest, it was uncomfortable, but here she was staring at a ringing phone and praying that she didn't have to push those feelings aside and pretend that friendship was all she felt for Sofiya.

Just before the call went to voicemail, a frazzled voice said "Hello?"

Molly wasn't sure whether to breathe a sigh of relief or hold her breath for the verdict. She dismissed the latter out of hand. This was sure to be a long conversation and while she had been feeling fluttery lately, she couldn't go fainting like an old-fashioned Victorian woman whose stays were too tight.

"Hey, Sarita, it's Sofiya. I've got Molly with me." Sofiya's voice was guarded and tight. Molly hated it. Judging by the pause on the other end of the line, Sarita didn't like it either.

"Hey, Sofiya. What's going on? I can't talk long. I've got my meeting with the board in just a few minutes."

"That's... actually what we wanted to talk to you about," Sofiya said, squeezing Molly's hand. Molly squeezed it back, hoping that it would help make this conversation easier. "Did you know that Chairman Dawes was in Richmond this week?"

There was another pause on the other end of the line, then Sarita spoke in a similarly tight tone of voice. "I found out late last night that he had taken a trip up there. How did *you* know that he was there?"

"Well, he was apparently staying in the hotel last night. He found us at breakfast this morning and gave us a nice little talking to."

Sarita groaned so loudly and at such a high pitch that it was almost a shriek. Molly was pretty sure she heard her stomping her feet, but she couldn't be sure.

"Of course he did. I knew I shouldn't have sent that video in. Ugh, I *knew* he'd get mad about it and take it out on someone who didn't deserve his wrath." Molly had to smother a laugh as her boss let loose a string of curses that told them both exactly what she thought of Chairman Dawes. Sofiya raised her eyebrows so high that they almost reached her blonde widows peak. After almost a full minute, she took a deep breath and continued speaking. "What did he have to say for himself? I assume there was a thinly veiled threat in his 'nice little talking to'?"

"Ah, you know him well," Molly quipped, belying the anxiety that had her stomach roiling. "I believe his exact words were 'If you keep fighting us on this, you are not going to like the results.'"

Sarita groaned again when Sofiya nodded and said, "That sounds about right."

"Well, the good news is, he doesn't have any hiring or firing power within the library. There's no way he can force me to fire you unless you've done something horrifically unethical in the three days you've been gone." She said it as if it was a foregone conclusion that there was no way that had happened.

"Well..." Molly trailed off, leaving plenty of space for another groan from Sarita to fill the room.

"Are you kidding me? Did you two decide *now* was the best time for you to finally act on all of the unresolved sexual tension that's been swirling between you since Molly started?"

Sofiya blushed, and Molly looked at her feet. It really was

terrible timing, as far as that was concerned. However, she was surprised to hear that Sarita didn't sound that upset outside of the groaning.

"Don't get me wrong," Sarita continued. "Inshallah, I'm excited that you two finally got your acts together and did something about it, but you know this means we all have *a lot* of paperwork to fill out as soon as you two get home? Like, we work for the government, but you should see the mess of paperwork we're going to go through..."

Sofiya and Molly looked at each other and burst into laughter as Sarita kept talking.

"Now, here's what you need to do to cover your asses," Sarita said seriously. They both listened carefully. Maybe this wasn't the end of the world -or their relationship- after all.

MOLLY

It was hard for Molly to get back into the swing of things for the conference when her head was so stuck on everything happening at home and her heart was wrapped up in everything to do with this relationship - and what that meant.

Molly was having a very hard time turning her brain off as she stood in signing lines to get some of the librarian's favorite books signed - including *Front Desk* by Kelly Yang for herself.

She hated that she couldn't stop thinking about the way

she felt about Sofiya. She'd felt some of it before in other relationships, but some of these feelings were brand new to her in their entirety. That made it hard for her to even think about talking about them to Sofiya.

What if she said the wrong thing and made Sofiya hate her? Or worse, what if she said everything that she was feeling and Sofiya realized just how different their emotions were about each other and decided that she wasn't worth the fuss? It wouldn't have been the first time. By the time she got to the front of the Yang signing line, she thought she was going to burst with everything she was holding in.

She handed her book over and said something that seemed appropriate, because Yang smiled, signed it to her and thanked her for coming. Molly ran away without saying anything else until she got to the hallway, which was blissfully -and surprisingly- empty. When her phone buzzed, she glanced at it and was surprised again to see Naomi's name and picture on the screen. It was an old photo where she had pressed her face up against the glass of a window to make it seem like she was trapped in the phone when it showed up. It was one of Molly's favorites,

Swiping to unlock it, she answered with a voice that trembled much more than she would have liked. "Hello?"

"Oh hey!" Naomi sounded surprised. "I didn't actually expect you to answer since you're at your fancy conference."

"Well, you got me," Molly replied. "What's up?

"Well, I was just gonna leave you a voicemail telling you I

love you and I hope you're having a bomb ass time! But I guess you get to hear me do that in person, now. Ha!"

Molly snorted a laugh. "I love you too, weirdo."

"So how come I get to talk to you in real time? I expected you to be having the time of your life hanging with all of your librarian buddies. Isn't Sofiya there with you?"

"Girl, this has been the weirdest conference in the history of all conferences, let me tell you. Actually, I have *so* much to tell you about everything that's happened."

"Well, I've got a little while before my next appointment, so spill." Molly could hear the squeak of Naomi's office chair, the one she had bought during their first semester of grad school and now refused to replace even though she had literally worn an ass print into the seat cushion. It was as reliable as Naomi was herself, and she loved them both.

"Where to even begin..." Molly thought out loud.

"How about the beginning?" Naomi suggested, using a tone of voice that Molly knew she used on her clients.

"Well, we almost wrecked on the way here and I spilled Dr. Pepper all down my front with an hour and a half to go on the drive, then broke down in front of Sofiya about how she must regret kissing a girl who couldn't even drive."

"Oh, Molly."

She filled her in on the rest, from the name tag mix up and the room change to the mind-blowing sex to the threat from Dawes and then the discussion with her boss. When she put it all out there at once, she wasn't surprised she was feeling so overwhelmed. It had been a *long* four days and she still wasn't done.

"So, first of all, congrats on the sex," Naomi said when she'd finished processing everything Molly had told her, "Second of all, want me to fuck up that chairman dude?"

The idea of five-foot nothing Naomi fighting Chairman Dawes made Molly burst into giggles. Maybe she was biased, but she would have put money on Naomi winning that fight. She was small, but she was scrappy.

"Not like, physically," Naomi laughed. "You know I don't fuck around with old racist white men. I can sic some of my lawyer friends on him, though."

"Well, hopefully that won't be necessary," Molly said soberly. "As long as he doesn't pull anything when we get home, we shouldn't *need* any lawyers."

"Well, good. Lawyers are a pain in the ass."

"Case in point," Molly laughed. Naomi joined in, her tinkling laugh making the world a little bit brighter. "But really, this week away from work has just been a lot."

"No kidding! Having sex with someone for the first time is a big deal all on its own, especially when you've been pining over them for the better part of a year!"

"I have not been pining!" Molly argued. "Pining over people is an alloromantic thing. I don't do that. I've just had a lot of sexual feelings. That's not the same thing."

"You may not have been pining by the strictest definition, but what you were doing was pretty similar to the sighing and wistful gazing that I do when I'm pining. It looks pretty similar from where I'm standing, though a lot less romantic."

"Wait, is that why I keep wishing I was holding her hand and daydreaming about spending days at her house playing with her cat?" She realized what she said and clapped a hand over her mouth. "Oh my god that was not meant to be as dirty as it sounded. She has an actual cat."

Naomi cackled. "Maybe you pine more than you think, in your own way. Romantic shit like that shows up out of nowhere sometimes. Especially after you've spent time playing with her... *cat*."

As much as Molly hated it, she had to admit that her best friend had a point, as usual. "Ugh. I had forgotten just how annoying romantic feelings were. And pervy best friends!"

Naomi ignored the last comment. "You think you're feeling them for Sofiya? It's been... what, six years?"

"Six years sounds about right," she mused as she counted backwards through her various relationships. Most of them had been purely sexual or friends with benefits situations. The last person she'd had romantic feelings for was one of her undergrad mates, Anna, and it was a relationship that had started with sparks in August and worked itself into a flame of emotions by Christmas, but been doused by her aro-phobia by graduation. It had been a while since she'd thought about her, but it still brought a twinge of sadness to remember how good things could have been if Anna hadn't been such an absolute asshole. "I don't know if they're really romantic yet. I really like her as a friend and the sex has been mind-blowing and I love spending time with her, but what if that's all I ever feel?"

"Well, she already knows that romantic feelings aren't a guarantee with you. You told her that from basically the very beginning of your friendship. Have you two talked about your expectations for the future?"

"Girl, when were we supposed to do that?" Molly rubbed the bridge of her nose. "We've barely managed to get through the stuff people paid a lot of money to send us to. And tonight there's the queer mixer thing that we both wanted to go to, to meet new people, but we haven't talked about how these changes have... well, changed those expectations either, and just... ugh."

"I know, boo. But it sounds like you need to talk to her about it. Communication really is key when you're trying to start something good, which I think is what's happening."

"Ugh," Molly groaned. "I don't know how y'all do this shit all the time. It's exhausting."

Naomi laughed again, not unkindly. "It's all about the hope that it'll be worth it in the long run, boo. Sofiya seems like good people, and you sound happy underneath all that stress. Am I reading you right?"

That brought a smile to her face. "You know what? I think you are. When did you get so smart?"

Underneath all the shit going on around her and Sofiya, she *was* happy. She had enjoyed every minute they'd spent together so far and she looked forward to whatever the two of them would do next. It had just taken a little bit of prodding from her best friend to truly realize it.

"Lots of practice, my love. Lots of practice. Now, I've got to go, but I hope you get to have some fun with your lady tonight at the mixer. Have the conversation when you're ready. I love you!"

"Love you, too, Naomi. Have a great afternoon!"

The phone beeped with the ended call and Molly looked at the time before sliding it back into her blazer pocket. It was almost 4, which meant that she had one more signing line to get in before the conference was essentially over. All that was left was the fun stuff. They could talk about the future on the ride home, or maybe another day. Right now, she was going to get ready to have a fun night with Sofiya. She wasn't going to let anything, not even her own feelings, get in the way of that.

SOFIYA

Sofiya had spent most of the day in panels, which had wrapped up in just enough time for her to come back to the room, shower and change into something a little bit more comfortable for a fun evening.

She stood in front of the bathroom mirror, having just finished re-styling her hair for the evening and was halfway through putting in a pair of gold arabesque earrings when Molly walked into the room carrying a very full tote that looked to be about half her body weight in books.

She took the bag and carried it to the armchair. She set it down with a loud grunt that brought a smile to Molly's face.

"Good lord! You're stronger than you look, missy," Sofiya said with a laugh. "How many books did you get signed? You were just complaining last week that you had no more shelf space to work with."

Her smile turned sheepish. "Well, I think 15 books by six different authors in there, but in my defense, only one of them is for me personally. One of these sets is for Savannah - she's a huge fan of Ilona Andrews' Kate Daniels series and I thought this would be the perfect birthday gift for her."

"Ah, so Savannah's a romance reader, huh? I knew I liked her. She's got good tastes," Sofiya declared, then wrapped her now-empty arms around her waist. "It's good to see you."

"You, too." She snuggled close and pressed her lips gently to Sofiya's. Sofiya loved the way it felt to have Molly's body pressed up against hers, their heartbeats racing together towards an unknown finish line.

"Are you changing for the mixer tonight?"

"I mean, I wasn't going to. Why? Is this too business-y?" She tugged at her blouse and bit the inside of her lip as she looked nervously down at Sofiya. It shouldn't have been a sexy expression, but as always when it came to Molly, she found everything she did sexy.

"No, you look wonderful. You always look wonderful," Sofiya reassured her, loving the way her face melted back into a smile. "I just didn't know if you needed me to get out of your hair to get ready or anything. I'm ready to go anyway."

Molly raised an eyebrow at her. "You sure about that, Sof?"

Frowning, Sofiya did a mental run through of everything she was wearing - dark wash skinny jeans, a black spaghetti strap tank top and a lightweight blue knit cardigan. Her hair was done and she just needed to refresh her lipstick to make her makeup perfect. She couldn't think of anything else that needed to happen before she left.

Sofiya looked up to see Molly standing in the bathroom with the earring dangling from her fingers. She reached up to her ear and laughed, feeling that, yes, there was only one earring there.

"I think you're going to want this." Molly smirked, twitching two fingers of her other hand to bring Sofiya to her. Sofiya crossed the room in three long strides and reached for the earring, only for it to be held just out of her reach. She reached again and was met with the same result, but her body was inches away from Molly's again. Her skin sang at the near contact.

"Allow me," Molly whispered. At Sofiya's nod, she used her free hand to tuck her hair behind her ear. With gentle fingers, she threaded the loop of the earring through the piercing and pressed a kiss to Sofiya's neck where it hung. A moan pulled itself from Sofiya's mouth. She turned her face to meet Molly's. Their lips collided as Molly kissed her back hungrily, more intensely than any of the kisses they had shared before. Sofiya wanted nothing more than to lose herself in the beauty of this moment, but before she could do any more than wrap her arms around her waist, Molly pulled back slightly, panting.

"If we keep going, we are going to be late for the mixer," she pointed out, voice rough. Sofiya hated to be late, but in this moment, she didn't care about the mixer. Her knees weakened at the thought of what they could do instead.

"Who gives a damn about the mixer?" Her frank statement came out in a growl. Molly's tongue darted out to lick her lips. "We'll go later. Right now, I just want you."

"Good. Because I have some *very* wicked plans for you."

Molly pushed her up against the counter, she spread her legs to accommodate the woman's wider body and was rewarded with a kiss that seared her to her soul.

"Turn around, Sofiya. I want you to see how beautiful you are when you're getting fucked."

Sofiya shivered at the growl of Molly's voice, and did as she was told. Molly trailed one manicured finger down her spine until she reached the place where the hem of her sweater met the waistband of her jeans. With a swift motion, she opens her jeans and lowers the zipper just enough to slip her graceful hand inside and run her finger along Sofiya's soaked satin underwear.

Sofiya moaned as her fingers brushed against her clit then dipped into her underwear. Every piece of skin she touched felt like it was on fire and she couldn't get enough. She anchored herself with her arms on the edges of the counter and tilted her hips to give Molly better access, hoping, praying that she would take the hint and give her some relief.

Fortunately, Molly's wicked plans apparently did involve relief. Unfortunately, she was taking her sweet time with it.

Sofiya loved every minute of it, rocking her body in rhythm with Molly's movements, gasping with pleasure so often that she almost couldn't breathe, and watching herself in the mirror. It was an exhilarating experience to watch yourself get fingered until you come. She loved the way that Molly's face was so focused, so determined on making sure she had as much pleasure as she physically could that she lit up with every sound Sofiya made.

Sofiya had never dreamed of having sex like this with anyone, but there was absolutely nothing like it. She loved watching herself come, as weird as that sounded.

If she was being honest, she loved Molly. She knew Molly wasn't ready to hear that, but it was the truth, and with every orgasm, she thought it as loudly as she could.

MOLLY

The flush of exertion and attraction had faded into a light blush on Sofiya's cheeks by the time they reached the ballroom. She had to give a nod to Bernard and his team of organizers - they had done a good job at transforming this room from a dining room to an exhibition hall and now into a proper dance floor.

There were quite a few people already dancing to a playlist blasting through the room, and Molly itched to join them. It wasn't the same as having an actual DJ, but she wanted to dance with Sofiya again. She didn't care if it was to a live band or someone's phone playing the radio.

With Sofiya's hand in hers, she knew that everything would be all right.

FEBRUARY 15

SOFIYA

Sofiya woke up in Molly's arms for the fourth day in a row, but for the first time, it didn't feel like a stolen moment. Instead, she just felt at home. It was one of those moments that she felt like she could experience every day for the rest of her life and it would still never feel commonplace. She didn't want to move a muscle, except to snuggle closer to Molly's still-sleeping chest, so that is exactly what she did. After all, it was the last day of the conference and they only had to go back home for an afternoon meeting with the Board of Supervisors. They had planned to grab breakfast and then spend some time at the two bookstores in town beforehand, but that could wait.

Last night had been everything Sofiya thought she had ever wanted, and yet she still wanted more. More of Molly, more of them together, more of this. Molly stirred in her sleep and tucked her bonneted head into Sofiya's shoulder with a soft murmur. Sofiya thought that it was probably the most adorable sound she had ever heard and snuggled closer. She was rewarded with the press of a light kiss to the top of her shoulder.

"G'morning." The husky tone of her sleep-heavy voice sent shivers down her spine.

"Good morning," Sofiya breathed. "Sleep well?"

Molly murmured an affirmative sound into her shoulder, pressing another kiss to the base of her neck. It was an echo of the first morning, but the words somehow had new depth to them that made them erotic, somehow. Or maybe that was just her dirty mind kicking into high gear from a gentle kiss.

She turned to face her and kissed her softly, but gently on the mouth. Molly responded with the same ardor she'd had the night before, which relieved Sofiya immensely.

"What do you say we delay our plans for a little while and get our morning off to a real good start?" Sofiya purred and was rewarded by Molly's beautiful brown eyes widening and darkening with what she could now clearly define as arousal. They were supposed to be at a meeting with Sarita and the Board of Supervisors in the afternoon, but that was ages away.

"I... I would like that," Molly stammered. "I would like that very much."

And so Sofiya got to work, if something so pleasurable could be considered work. She trailed kisses from the base of her silk bonnet until she reached the buttoned front of her nightgown. Unbuttoning it one by one, she let her mouth travel along the same path from collarbone to navel until it was entirely undone and she could see almost all of her long, beautiful body.

Molly had magnificent breasts, which was something that Sofiya had obviously noticed before. But with them right in front of her, they were just large enough to mound in her hand with brown nipples that were erect and waiting to be touched. It didn't take long for Sofiya to free them entirely from the cotton gown and began to play with them. She traced circles around the nipple on one while she stroked her thumb over the other. Molly arched her back pressing harder against Sofiya and Sofiya took the hint.

She pressed herself against Molly, wrapping her arms around her curvy body. Rolling them both so she straddled Molly's hips, she removed her own nightgown with a fluid movement.

"Now, tell me how you like it," Sofiya commanded. And Molly was only too happy to show her.

SOFIYA

By the time they made it out of bed, they were pushing the deadline to check out, even though the staff had been gracious enough to delay it on account of the changed arrangements. Sofiya had never been so grateful for a late check out in her life. Getting to spend more time getting to know Molly was something she was pretty sure she would never turn down again, now that she'd been given the chance to get started.

Each of them ran around the room, collecting all of the things they had used. It was amazing just how many of their belongings had been strewn about the room over the previous three days, considering they were both otherwise fairly clean people.

Molly was the first one finished, so she did one last walk through of the bedroom and bathroom and came back with an armful of Sofiya's travel-sized bottles from the shower. Sofiya grimaced, realizing she'd forgotten them. She pulled out the zippered plastic carrying case she had flattened underneath her clothes and Molly dropped them in.

"That's everything, so I'm gonna head down and start the checkout process, okay?"

Sofiya nodded and Molly pressed a quick kiss to her lips before grabbing her suitcase and speed-walking to the door. She couldn't help but watch the sway of her hips as she walked, which is why she caught the glint of a grin when she tossed one last sentence over her shoulder.

"Don't take too long, dear. I might just leave without you."

Sofiya rolled her eyes and kept rolling her clothes so that they would fit back in the suitcase well enough to make it home and into her laundry machine.

Before long she was finished. She looked around the room, from the rumpled bed to the bathroom hamper full of used towels. She couldn't believe that just four days ago, she had thought of this room as sterile, as somewhere where you wouldn't be able to make any decent new memories.

Ridiculous as it was, she almost wanted to take the room home with her and ensure that these memories never faded. But then the hotel would charge the library and then Sarita would know just how much of a sentimental fool she was under her tailored pantsuits and mock her mercilessly. As she would deserve. Instead, she drank in the way she felt in the room and did the best she could to commit it to memory before zipping up her suitcase and rolling it out of the room behind her.

MOLLY

Molly was finished checking out of the room by the time Sofiya made it to her at the front desk.

She smiled as the older woman walked slowly over to her, putting a little bit more swing than usual into it. Molly didn't think she would ever get tired of watching the way she moved. She greeted her with a swift kiss when she reached her, only to be interrupted again.

"Well, fancy meeting you two here again," a now too-familiar voice drawled. Molly had to hold in a scream. The man just would not go away!

"Now, I could have sworn when I asked that you said you two weren't together. Were you telling an old man a falsehood?" His tone was ponderous, but his eyes were as cold as any snakes. "I am not a fan of being lied to, ladies."

Sofiya reached over and gave her hand a squeeze before looking at Mr. Dawes.

"Mr. Dawes, we are not a fan of being threatened for doing our jobs the way we see fit. Would you just go out of your way to tell a man who threatens to get you fired that, oh yeah, you're a lesbian and dating your coworker?"

Molly was proud that her voice didn't tremble a bit, despite the fact that she was standing up to a man who terrified her.

"Well, if you weren't ashamed of your sexualities, then why did you try to hide it from me?

"Because you are technically one of our bosses. Because you're a known homophobe and a racist. Because it's none of your damn business who we date!" Sofiya yelled. "Take a pick of any of those reasons!"

The sound of her words echoed across the room, and she flushed a bright red from the tips of her ears all the way down the back of her neck. Molly couldn't tell if it was from anger or embarrassment, but her heart glowed with pride for her girlfriend. She was absolutely right. Molly squeezed her hand and stepped even closer to her. Dawes was standing there with his mouth wide open, like the toad he was.

"Now, we are leaving to go home and attend that stupid meeting with all of you. We will see you there with our boss and the rest of the county administration employees, all of whom now know about the threat you made. So, you will have to excuse us."

Without waiting for an answer, she stalked towards the front door, rolling her suitcase behind her. She turned to follow, when she heard her name being called.

"Ms. Andersen! Wait!"

Turning around again, Dawes was still rooted to the spot. Behind him, Bernard was walking faster than she thought was possible and waving a sheet of paper at her.

When he caught up to her, he was slightly out of breath but he shoved two pages into her hands.

"We need you to fill these out and send them back in. They're satisfaction surveys and they are vital to making this convention a better place next year!"

Molly just laughed and walked out the door behind Sofiya, leaving the two men to do whatever the hell they pleased.

SOFIYA

Sofiya made it to the car just in time for the shock to wear off and the horrific anxiety and embarrassment to set in. She had yelled at the Chairman of the Board and told him exactly what she had always thought of him and then just walked away.

Plus, she didn't have the keys to the car. All she could do was stand next to the hybrid looking ridiculous until

Molly came out to let her in, replaying everything that had happened in her head. If she hadn't been worried about her job before, there was certainly reason to be worried now. She also hadn't done the library any favors by pissing off a man who already didn't like any of the work they did. It made her stomach churn, thinking of everything she could have ruined with just a few sentences.

Luckily, she didn't have to wait too long. She heard Molly's deep laugh before she saw her, which did a little to ease the tension in her chest. If she was laughing like that, then maybe her outburst hadn't been as bad as she thought.

Molly turned the corner and walked towards her with her suitcase in one hand and what looked like paper in the other, but with a wide smile on her face that brought out a matching one on Sofiya's.

"Well, you certainly told him what you thought of him," Molly remarked. "Did it make you feel better?"

"Uh, no. I'm so anxious I could vomit," she said tightly. "I very well might have ruined our chances at getting the library funding kept level. If he's feeling particularly crotchety, we might even get a larger budget cut.

"Hey, it'll be okay," Molly reassured her. "He already wasn't going to help us out, so you probably didn't do much damage. Nothing you said was untrue, even if he'll try to claim he isn't sexist or racist. Anybody with a lick of sense can see that."

That did make Sofiya feel a little bit better. She wasn't

alone in her hatred for the man, and maybe she hadn't ruined everything.

Pressing a button on her key fob, her trunk popped open just enough for Sofiya to lift it. She shoved her dark blue suitcase in and took Molly's from her. She was a little gentler with the lavender case, conscious that it wasn't hers to beat the hell out of. When she turned around, Molly was still holding the paper in her hand.

"What's that? Did Dawes give you something?"

"No, this was freakin' Bernard," she laughed, waving the paper at Sofiya. "Before I could walk out behind you, he came hollering after me with these in his hands. They're *satisfaction surveys*."

That startled a laugh from Sofiya. "Wow, that is really something. I'll give him one thing - he never gives up. He messes up our name tags, messes up our room arrangements, begs me to do a panel at the last minute and then actually *wants* us to do a satisfaction survey? Does he think we're going to give him a great review?"

"Oh, it wasn't all bad," Molly grinned, taking a step towards Sofiya and closing the trunk. "After all, we finally got together thanks to his mistakes. I think we can give him a little bit of a break, don't you?"

Sofiya smiled back, and brushed a kiss across her lips. "Mmmm maybe. I'll think about it while I nap on the way home."

MOLLY

The drive home was entirely uneventful and full of traffic in a way it hadn't been when they had gone in the other direction. They arrived at the county administration half an hour before the meeting was due to start, and saw Sarita pacing the length of the building's lobby through the windows.

As she shifted the car into park, the butterflies of her nerves began to flutter through her stomach. She knew that she had no reason to be nervous. There was no way that Dawes would pull anything in a meeting that was recorded and uploaded to the internet in three different places. Not to mention, there was guaranteed to be at least one reporter there. She was pretty sure that the Register hadn't replaced their county reporter after she was hired as part of the community college's public relations team. Even then, Fiona from the Star Tribune was a fabulous reporter. Since she had been dating her counterpart at the Register for nearly a year, Molly knew that she wouldn't let any blatant homophobia slip through her fingers. And, hopefully, that would make all the difference.

Sarita's face brightened when she saw them pushing through the double doors.

"Oh, good, you made it back okay! Welcome home, lovebirds!"

Molly laughed sheepishly and bumped her hip against Sofiya's. "We're sorry our timing sucks."

Sarita tsked, still smiling. "Timing is never going to be

good, but I'm glad you two are happy. Now, we are first up on the agenda, so hopefully we can get out of here before these men bore everyone to tears. Are you ready for the presentation?"

"There's only so ready we can get." Sofiya shrugged, about summing up what Molly was thinking.

"I'm pretty sure that we'll be able to handle whatever they want to throw at us."

"Good, because as soon as we're done, you both get to go talk to human resources and fill out their piles of paperwork regarding the relationship changes."

Molly's heart sank. She had known it would need to happen, but she'd hoped it would wait until Monday when she was back at work. Although, she realized, she was technically back on the clock now, so it made sense. The county would want to cover its ass and adhere to their new policy, and she understood that, but it was always scary to get summoned to talk to HR. Especially when she already knew exactly what she'd done wrong, and how entirely right it had turned out for them both. She could only tell the truth and they would just have to deal with the consequences. Looking at Sofiya and the way her steady eyes brought her more comfort than she could have imagined, she knew they could weather whatever HR had to throw at them.

Before she could answer Sarita, though, Chad Dawes walked in again. He glared at the three women standing together as he passed them and headed into the boardroom. She barely held back a groan as Sarita raised her eyebrows at them both.

"What on earth happened there? Did you guys get into it again?"

Sofiya filled her in on the morning's argument and was rewarded with a look of absolute disgust on her face. Molly loved how their boss was always on their side, even when it made things harder for her to do her job.

"Why the hell was he in Richmond again? Well, I guess we know why he was late. He was supposed to be here an hour ago." She pressed her lips together and looked at her watch. "And now if we're not careful, we'll be late to this one while we stand here and gab. Let's head on in and get set up."

The butterflies came back in full force, but Molly had Sofiya and their fantastic boss. With the both of them beside her, there was very little in the world that could actually harm her. She strode into the room with confidence, ready to show off the work she was very proud of and make her case for avoiding another budget cut.

They seated themselves in the front row of folding chairs next to the county's treasurer and waited. The meeting was called to order shortly thereafter and after going over the agenda, it was their turn to present to the board.

Sarita walked up to the podium and they followed after here so they could all address the old white men sitting at the conference table.

"Good afternoon, gentlemen. We are here today to present our budgetary needs and make our case for keeping our funding level. We know that the budget is tight, as it always is, and you must make smart financial decisions. In order to help you do that, I have broken down all of our expenditures as well as our income in things like late fees and printer usage. You can see all of the data for the last three years in your board packet, along with a general overview.

Each of the board members flipped a few pages in the spiral bound books before them and Molly could see the pie charts and tables showing everything they'd spent money on.

"As you can see," Sarita continued. "Our expenditures are quite low. Over the last five years we have lowered our costs on purchasing books and other services by working in tandem with other libraries in our region. We've also lowered our up-front costs on digital services like Hoopla and Overdrive by negotiating with our distributors and finding alternate ways to ensure that our readers have access to everything they need. On the next page, you'll also see that late fees are up as well as printer charges and book sales, though those are not a large income source whatsoever. Do you have any questions?"

Several board members did, asking why certain costs had gone up over the years. Sarita answered them honestly. The truth was that services were getting more expensive. That was just the way the world worked at the moment, and they had to figure out which services they needed to make the library run. When they were out of questions, it was Molly and Sofiya's turn to speak.

"When we heard there was another proposed budget cut, we decided to do what we could to help you see how the library services affect the people of this county," Molly said, proud that her voice was steady. "Sofiya and I made a video with short interviews that will show you exactly who uses the libraries and why they believe that our work is valuable. We hope that this will help you to make an informed decision on what funding goes to when it gets into our fantastic director's hands. And I personally hope you enjoy it."

The video began to play, and all three women walked back to their seats to await any further questions. The board members had none, though Molly suspected there would be questions later on. They had done everything they could, and it was time for them to go talk to HR. For the first time since Sarita had told her about it, Molly felt ready to have the conversation she needed to have - both with Sofiya and with the HR rep.

SOFIYA

Sofiya had been the first one to talk to HR and was then sent home so that Molly could speak to them on her own. Sofiya was so glad to be at home again. Being in her own space with her own cat was a priceless feeling. Everything was right where it should be, except that she kept wanting to turn and say something to someone who wasn't.

It was like the ghost of Molly was following her around the same way Luke did as she cooked herself some tomato soup and a grilled cheese. Sitting down at the kitchen table, she felt alone in her house for the first time in recent memory, and she did not like that feeling. Claudia was already back at their own home, probably enjoying being back in their own space, too. She didn't want to call them and make them feel like they had to come over, because she was a grown woman. Sofiya had always been perfectly fine in her own space before. She would be fine on her own again. She had only been home for the better part of two hours. It was ridiculous to be lonely already. Wasn't it?

"It's ridiculous to miss her already, isn't it?" Sofiya posed the question to Luke, knowing that he had no opinion on the subject. He chirped at her happily, then pawed at her plate. She laughed at him and tugged the grilled cheese a little further out of his reach. He meowed at her again in retaliation. With a smile, she scratched between his ears until he crawled into her laps and succumbed to purrs. "Who's a good kitty?"

He really was a good cat, but the lonely feeling did not abate. She longed to see Molly again, ached to hold her in her arms. She was going to at least invite her over. The worst that could happen would be that she said no, and at best, they'd get to spend the night together again. Either way, she'd have her answer.

She picked up her phone and tapped out a quick text.

"The sunset is beautiful tonight. Want to come watch it with me?"

Before a minute had passed, there was a return text.

"I was just thinking about you. Be there in five."

A grin spread across her face. Molly had been thinking about her, too. She dug into her food with more gusto than before and put her kettle on to boil some water for cocoa. No February sunset-watching session was complete without hot cocoa and a blanket.

Just in time for her to finish her dinner, three knocks sounded at the door. Luke dashed towards it, purring all the way as if he could open it on his own and greet guests. When she opened the door, Molly stood there with the setting sun lighting her from behind, making her look like the goddess she was.

"Honey, I'm home," she quipped and Sofiya pulled her in for a kiss. Finally, it felt like home again.

MOLLY

They settled onto the swing that took up much of the front porch, complete with steaming mugs of hot cocoa, a blanket covering their laps and Luke twining around their legs. It was peaceful, probably the first peaceful moment they'd spent together. There was nowhere to go. No one else needed them, except for the cat who was always in need of attention, and everything felt right.

She itched to tell her about everything that had happened since they'd last spoken this afternoon. Everything that had happened over the last week had happened just so quickly that she didn't want to ruin the first real moment of peace that they had had together. So she waited, watching the pink of the sunset turn to deep red and then to dark blue while she snuggled up against Sofiya. The night would have been absolutely perfect, if not for the niggling worry at the back of her mind. She had to say something, and as the last of the color dipped behind the trees, she knew it had to be now.

"You know, the HR rep asked me a question today that I didn't have an answer to." Her voice was measured, as if it wasn't that big of a deal.

"Oh, I believe that. I feel like half of their job is asking questions that we have to soul search to answer," Sofiya laughed. "What did they ask you?"

"They asked me where I saw this relationship going in the future," she said slowly. Over the lip of her mug, she could see Sofiya go still. "I told them I had to think about that, then talk to you about it.

"I see. What are you thinking, then?"

Molly couldn't tell what Sofiya was thinking from the expression on her face, but the way she rubbed at the band of her watch told her that she was nervous. At least that made two of them, she thought as her heart thundered in her chest. Molly took a long drink of the hot chocolate she held in her hands before she answered in a serious voice.

"I think we both have to talk about our expectations, because feelings are complicated and I don't want either of us to get hurt."

"Feelings can be complicated, yeah. I'd think that mine were pretty clear by now, though." Sofiya's voice trembled a little. "I want this relationship to continue to grow into something.

Molly grimaced. "Well, that's the thing. This kind of relationship has gone badly for me in the past, especially when I've started developing feelings for the person in them. It's part of why I avoided you after you kissed me."

Sofiya perked up, like a cat who had heard their human opening a can of wet food. "You've developed feelings for me?

Molly held out a hand to Sofiya and she took it in hers. Sofiya rubbed circles with the pads of her thumb

"I care about you a lot. You know that romantic love is something that doesn't come easily for me, but I think that it very well could be love someday. And I needed you to know that before this went any further. I needed us both to be on the same page."

Sofiya grinned so widely it looked like she was about to burst. "Molly, I've been falling in love with you since the very day you walked into the library. Didn't you know that?"

"And it's not a problem for you that I might not ever fall in love with you?" Molly asked, looking into Sofiya's steady blue eyes and trying to keep herself from crying. "That I might not ever return your feelings? That it might be months or years before anything changes? Don't you want more from this?"

"I want to share my life with *you*, Molly. Whatever parts of yourself that you are willing or able to share with me. Does that make sense?"

Molly nodded. She had lost the battle to keep herself composed, but she didn't care. She set down her mug and let Sofiya take hold of her other hand.

"We have great chemistry and we're great friends and it

will be what it will be in the end. All I need from you is your company and a willingness to keep spending time with me. Everything else, we can figure out along the way. Deal?"

"Deal."

MAY 22

SOFIYA

The final budget meeting was taking approximately seventeen years, and Sofiya couldn't stand it. She sat right next to Molly and gripped her hand as tightly as she could while her leg shook with anxiety. The board had privately committed to keeping the library's budget as it had been the year before, and it was written into the one that had gone forward for public consumption, but she didn't trust any of them as far as she could throw them - something she absolutely couldn't do with any of the men in front of her. It was especially true because she could feel Chairman Dawes' baleful glare directed at her and Molly every time he remembered they were there, which was relatively often because there were only maybe thirty people spread across the auditorium.

It probably should have bothered her that his hatred for her was so blatant, but there were more important things at hand to worry about. Besides, with Molly's hand in hers, there was very little that could cause them harm. It had been more than three months since the conference and Sofiya couldn't be happier. They spent nearly every non-working hour and a good chunk of the working ones together. She never tired of seeing her or spending time with her, and she couldn't wait until this meeting was over so she could kiss her senseless and celebrate this win.

Soon after the meeting was opened, people began to be called one by one to give the speeches they prepared. Each person spoke about something different - one thanked them for not raising taxes to pay for "ridiculous things like teaching kids to cook," while another told them they should be ashamed of themselves for making county employees work twice as hard for a third of the money as they had three years ago. At that, there were cheers from some of the people she recognized as county employees in the crowd and boos from some of the Republicans in the back. It was impossible to please everyone in such a polarized county, but Sofiya was glad that the cheers overpowered the boos. It was good to know that some people appreciated what they did. Finally, her name was called and Molly squeezed her hand as she made her way to the front.

"Hello, everyone. My name is Sofiya Anderson and I'm the reference librarian for all of Pittsylvania County. I just want to thank the board for listening to all of the wonderful residents of our county and remembering how important a library is to giving every person in our county a better quality of life, from the kids we teach about cooking to the county employees who get to be a part of something great."

She heard titters behind her at the pointed remark, but focused her eyes on the older men that sat at the front of the room. There were no smiles on their faces despite the fact that she was complimenting them on being decent humans.

"You have made a huge difference in the lives of every single person you represent, and even if they're mad about the money, they'll all be better off for it. So thank you."

Turning away from the podium, she walked back to where her girlfriend sat, beaming, in the second row. She had done everything she could and spoken for the library and the county, and it would have to be enough. All that was left was the board's vote.

"Thank you all for your time speaking to us tonight," the county administrator said evenly. "Ms. Anderson was the last person on our list to speak, so now it is time for the board members to cast their votes. This will be a roll call vote. When I call your name, please vote yes or no to accept the full budget as advertised."

Sofiya held her breath while one by one, the administrator called each of the board members' names and heard their answers. Every single one of them voted yes. Even Chairman Dawes, who looked like he'd bitten into something sour.

She had to resist the urge to scream with delight when the budget was officially passed and the meeting ended. The board members wouldn't take kindly to that, and neither would the Sheriff's deputies in charge of keeping the peace. Instead, she wrapped Molly up in her arms and squeezed her as tight as she could. She couldn't wait to get back to the library to tell everyone the good news.

MOLLY

Molly let out a delighted scream the instant they left the confines of the courthouse, and Sofiya joined her in it, spinning her around with a look of absolute joy on her face, then pulled her into a kiss that took her breath away.

They had done it. Through all of the bullshit with the recording and Chairman Dawes and the rest of the board members, they had succeeded in doing exactly what they had set out to do and now they were going to go celebrate with all of their friends and coworkers. Even though they'd spent nearly two hours in the stiff, uncomfortable chairs of the local courthouse, this was shaping up to be a fantastic evening.

They walked back to the library hand-in-hand, passing the small local goods store and the now-closed Crescent. Sofiya hummed a little tune as their hands swung, then spoke for the first time since leaving.

"I'm not ready for tonight to be over," she murmured, barely loud enough for Molly to hear her.

"Good thing we're headed to a party, then, isn't it?" Molly teased, bumping her with her hip. Sofiya flashed her a grin and bumped her back.

"That's not what I mean. I don't want to go back to my house alone tonight. It just... doesn't feel right."

Molly knew what she meant. Now that she'd had a taste of spending every night beside Sofiya, she hated the two or three nights a week that she spent alone in her own bed. It was an extremely comfortable mattress and she loved it, but there was nothing quite as soothing as sleeping next to the woman she adored.

"I can spend the night tonight, if you want. I just have to swing by my place and grab a new outfit for tomorrow."

"No, that's not what I mean." Sofiya closed her eyes and slowed to a halt on the sidewalk. "I don't want you to have to go home and grab clothes when you spend the night. I don't want it to be 'spending the night.'"

Molly's eyes widened. "What do you mean? What are you asking?"

"I'm tired of splitting our time between two houses that are five minutes away from each other. I want us to move in together. I don't care if it's into your place or mine or we find someplace that's entirely ours. I don't care where we are, as long as we're together."

Molly felt her eyes welling with tears -happy ones- and she laughed. "Oh, Sofiya. Of course we can move in together. You're my family. You and Luke."

That made Sofiya laugh, too, and the sound warmed Molly from the tips of her toes all the way to the roots of her hair. She was pretty sure she would never get tired of that sound, and she couldn't wait to test that theory.

THE END

AROMANTIC RESOURCES

As you likely know, I am not aromantic. I can fall in love at the drop of a hat and fall out of love just as quickly. Because of that and because many people are not as informed as they could be on what aromanticism is, I wanted to offer some resources and other people that you can read aromantic stories from.

AROMANTIC AUTHORS TO READ

For those of you searching for aromantic characters in other books, please check out Claudie Arseneault's Aro-Ace Database, and check out the authors below. All of them have publicly identified as somewhere on the aromantic spectrum, so you are more likely to get an ownvoices take on their identities.

- Laura Pohl
- Xan West
- Rosiee Thor
- Ashia Monet

- Claudie Arseneault
- Michelle Kan
- Emily Skrutskie
- Penny Stirling
- E.H. Timms
- Polenth Blake
- Lynn E. O'Connacht
- RoAnna Sylver
- Darcie Little Badger
- Michon Neal

I have also written two other books with aromantic characters as Ceillie Simkiss - *An Unexpected Invitation* and *Pack Ties*.

RESOURCES ON AROMANTICISM

- AUREA (aromanticism.org);
- Asexuality Visibility and Education Network (aven.org);
- Lynn O'Connacht's Youtube series about aromantic representation in fiction;
- aromantic.lgbt - this tumblr has a lot of good resources available and is the current host for Aromantic Spectrum Awareness Week.

For those of you reading in print, you can visit candaceharperauthor.com/aromantic-resources to read this with the links intact.

ACKNOWLEDGMENTS

I had the idea for this book a few months before I started writing it. I was inspired by a tweet about librarians and a prompt for only one bed, and thus Mrs. Mix Up was born.

To all the folks in Pittsylvania County that accidentally stumble upon this, sorry not sorry for taking liberties with Chatham and the politics there. It's all for a good purpose, I swear.

Mom and Dad, if you're reading this, please never ever tell me. Now that we're past the true embarrassment of you reading something I wrote sex scenes in, I am so eternally grateful for you telling me to always be myself and to "go write something really gay" when I lost my main source of income. It meant more to me than you will probably ever know. Because, again, you are never allowed to read this.

I'd like to give a shout out to my roommate and my husband for allowing me to wander around the apartment asking weird questions that were only occasionally plot-relevant. Thank you so much for being the main components of my Seattle-ish family.

I'd like to say thank you to all of the people who encouraged me to keep writing this even when it ballooned from a short story to a novelette to the novel you see before you. To everyone on Twitter, in various writing groups, and in real life, thank you.

In more specifics, though, I'd like to thank X and Lina for their unending support and teaching me so many great things about the business and craft of being an author. Amara, Clarissa, Corey, and Abigail, thank you so much for keeping me company for so much of the writing process. Thank you all for being around while I waffled about how I wanted a scene to go, or looking at my very vague outline and saying "hey, there's a good story there!"

And last but not least, to my readers. I got so much more attention for this book than I expected and I am both thrilled and terrified to hear what you thought of it.

ABOUT THE AUTHOR

Candace Harper is a queer, neurodivergent woman living with her partner, two cats and a dog in the PNW. She's known for being the overly enthusiastic about silly things and as the "mom friend." She writes queer fiction as much and in as many genres as she can manage, both under this name and as Ceillie Simkiss.

To keep up with her work, the best places to go are her newsletter and her twitter!

 facebook.com/candaceharperauthor

 twitter.com/_candaceharper

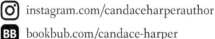 instagram.com/candaceharperauthor

bookbub.com/candace-harper

CPSIA information can be obtained
at www.ICGtesting.com
Printed in the USA
LVHW051746040820
662391LV00015B/1659